ENTHRALLED BY YOU

ANGELA PEARSE

Set in Mick Caster and Sabon.
Cover art by My Lan Khuc Valle (www.laolanart.com)

ISBN 978-1-914531-72-9 Paperback (KDP)
ISBN 978-1-914531-73-6 Paperback (IngramSpark)

Author Note

Enthralled By You is a light-hearted paranormal romance, but it does contain some darker elements related to vampirism. These include biting, exsanguination, bloodplay, violence, bloodshed, animal death (off-page), self-harm, and lack of bodily autonomy due to enthrallment. The story also features on-page sexual content. Please be mindful if you are sensitive to these themes.

Chapter 1

Sadie | London, 1758

The gentleman isn't one of my regulars. But he paid up front, is well dressed, and handsome to boot. His lengthy rod, once he removes his breeches, is an extra treat; and it doesn't take much licking and teasing on my part to get it nice and stiff. Luckily for him. His appointment is for fifteen minutes only, and I've got a regular waiting downstairs. Then again, gentlemen who need extra foreplay to get them ready for the sack will pay double and don't seem too bothered about forking it over.

And so they should. I'm a popular girl at Fanny Swift's elegant establishment in Covent Garden, so I'm never short of business. All the high-ranking toffs know I'm value for money, and this one asked for me by name, so I must have been recommended. Or he's read about me in *Harris's List*: *Sadie Smith, 21, silky blonde hair and luscious long legs. You won't get much conversation, but you'll get a fast sweet fuck.*

This gentleman is certainly delivering the goods in that respect. I'm on my back (where you can usually find me of an eve) with my yellow silk dress rucked up round my thighs and enjoying a right good rogering. But beneath the thud of the headboard and the gentleman's grunts comes the quick patter of feet and hushed voices.

I lift my head off the pillow, listening acutely.

'Wait, wait,' I gasp. 'There's something happening in the hallway. It could be a raid.'

I'm wary of raids. I only escaped one earlier in the month by the skin of my teeth. 'Get off me. I don't want to end up in the Clink.'

The gentleman thrusts his hips faster. 'Excuse my French, but quite frankly, fuck the raid,' he pants. 'I'm too close to stop now. And if I don't finish, you don't get paid.'

The pretty pile of silver coin stacked on the dresser seems to wink at me, and I bite my lip, not wanting to give it back. But the constables could burst through the door at any minute, and I'll be arrested.

'Hurry up then.' I squeeze my cunny round his sliding cock and circle my hips. That always helps things along.

The gentleman groans and immediately pumps his load. Thank the sweet Lord! As soon as he pulls out, I'm off the bed and swiping the coins into my drawstring purse. The pattering feet outside my door have now turned into pounding ones and are punctuated by distant squeals and shouts. It's definitely a raid, a bad one.

'*Fuck!*' I hastily stuff my feet into my shoes.

'Is there a back way out?' asks the gentleman nonchalantly, shrugging on his jacket. He doesn't seem at all bothered by the threat of the raid. Then again, he's a man, and they'll turn a blind eye to him. Even more if he's wealthy, he can dole out some coin and be on his way. It's worse for me. I could be whipped, put in the pillory, or sent to the Clink; and I don't fancy beating hemp.

'Yes, come on!' I push him out the door ahead of me. Scantily clad women and men with their breeches flapping are sprinting down the hallway towards the secret backstairs. I risk a glance over the railing and see several dark coats milling about. A door bangs, followed by female squeals, then men shouting and loud foul-mouthed cursing. My heart jumps into my mouth. They're clearing the downstairs first. But my luck might hold again tonight. If we're quick.

Joining the fast-moving current of escapees, we all clatter down the rickety stairs. No doubt, Fanny (aka Mother Swift), true to her name, will have already made her hasty getaway down them and run off to her sister's. The warm night flows over my sweaty skin as we burst out into the dank narrow alleyway at the back of the house. My gentleman is jostled in the panicked throng, but he remembers his manners and politely doffs his hat to me.

'Thank you for a pleasant evening, Sadie. I hope we'll meet again. Under less ... fraught circumstances.'

I incline my head and drop a curtsy, my full coin purse whacking my hip. He's generous, so he can definitely go on my list of regulars.

He turns on his heel and is swallowed up by the night, and I stroll in the opposite direction, heading for the local pub. The girls and I will chat and sympathise over who's been nabbed and count our lucky stars it wasn't us.

Alone in the alleyway, I lean against the brick wall for a breather and to repin my hair. What a night! My heart is going like the clappers. I'm not sure I can stand any more of these raids. They seem to be getting worse. I squat, have a relieved piss against the wall, and continue on my way. I'm passing by a narrow alleyway leading off to the right when a deep, smooth male voice says, 'Good evening,' from the depths.

I stop, startled, and peer in. But it's as black as pitch, and I can't see anyone.

'Hello?'

There's a scuffling noise, and I glimpse a sudden movement, but nothing that can be discerned or that could be called a man.

'Do not be alarmed,' says the voice.

'I'm not,' I reply. 'What do you want?'

There's a pause. 'How much for your services?'

Oho, so that's why he's lurking around the back of the brothel. He sounds posh. I could have a quickie in the alleyway before I get to the pub and add some more coin to my purse.

'Depends. Suck or fuck?' I ask.

There's another pause and a slight cough, as if I've been too direct.

'Would you consider coming to my house? I'll pay you well for your time.'

'Perhaps,' I reply coyly. 'Where is it?'

'Not too far from here. A five-minute stroll.'

I hesitate. Mother Swift doesn't like us going to gentlemen's homes in case their wives are out visiting—it causes unnecessary drama if they find out later, and she likes to run a calm establishment.

'Are you married?'

'No, I am not.'

'Well, I suppose that would be all right.' I have a couple of hours up my sleeve before it's safe to return.

'Shall we then?'

In the slice of moonlight illuminating the alleyway, I see a large hand with long fingers encased in black leather extending from the shadows.

Above the glove is a sliver of pale skin and a snake tattoo winding around his forearm. Hmm, he seems intriguing. I wonder if his cock is also tattooed with a snake. If it is, the girls would love to hear about that.

Smiling to myself, I slide my hand into his and walk into the dark alleyway without a second thought.

CHAPTER 2

Sadie | Edinburgh, present day

Blood. There was so much blood. All over me. The last thing I remember is screaming at Hester and Floss. After that, I must have passed out as I've come to on my bedroom floor. Concerned voices are discussing me overhead.

'She's fainted from shock.'

'We need to get this blood off her.'

'I'll clean up in here.'

I'm carried into the bathroom and bundled into the tub like a doll, fully clothed. The shower starts up, and I'm doused in a warm spray of water from the handheld nozzle. Blood sluices off me. *His* blood. I sit there, watching, unmoving, as Elliott is washed down the plughole. I think I moan a little, I'm not sure. This all seems surreal. There's a buzzing in my head, and I don't know what it means. My head lolls back against the wall. I just want to sleep.

'Sadie,' a voice says sharply, jolting me out of my dazed

state; and I jerk upright. Hester is kneeling beside me with the shower nozzle. 'I need to get your clothes off,' she says gently. 'Will you let me do that?'

She looks worried, like I might bite her if she touches me. I nod, feeling like my brain belongs to someone else. Hester leans me forward and tugs my crop top over my head and unhooks my bra. They're chucked down the end of the bath. My white T-shirt and lace bra are a mottled pink colour. Hester is now attempting to pull down my skirt, and I come to a little more, realising I'm about to be naked with an audience. I glance behind Hester, but it's just her and me in the bathroom. My blood-splattered denim skirt joins the rest of my clothes at the end of the tub with a squelch. Hester doesn't comment on the fact I'm not wearing knickers. I never do when Elliott comes over. *Don't think about what happened.* I drag my attention back to Hester with an effort.

'Where are the others?'

'Floss is finding Damian something to wear. She flew him over to ours in a T-shirt and boxers, and he was freezing since we don't use central heating.'

Floss's fragile little human dentist. My gut twists in resentment. *If she hadn't gotten involved with him, then Elliott wouldn't have been dragged off by Alexander*, I think to Hester. I know that doesn't make logical sense, but I need someone to blame.

Hester squirts shampoo on my hair and scrubs at my scalp. Pink suds trickle down over my breasts. *Elliott was just in the wrong place at the wrong time*, she replies, rinsing out the shampoo. I shut my eyes tightly and give my head a shake. That buzzing noise is really irritating.

Hester combs conditioner none too gently through my hair, and I hiss in pain when the comb snags. I hate people playing with my hair! Elliott is the only one I let touch it.

'Sorry,' she says out loud and combs more carefully.

I rub my temple distractedly as the buzzing intensifies. It feels like I've got bees flying around in my brain. Hester helps me out of the tub and wraps me in a black fluffy towel. She sees me looking at my bloody clothes in the tub.

'I'll get rid of them,' she says.

'Thanks,' I say gruffly.

'Do you need help getting dressed or ...?'

'I'm OK.'

Hester: *Come out to the lounge when you're ready. I'll have a little cup of something warmed and ready for you.*

I balk at that, knowing that it's going to be some of the fresh blood supply Elliott dropped off earlier this evening. It'll remind me of him.

Me: *I've lost my appetite.*

Hester: *You need to feed. Just a little. To keep your*

strength up.

Me: *Fine.*

Alone in my room, I curl up on the bed, nosing for Elliott's scent on the pillow. But someone has stripped and remade it since it was streaked with arterial blood. It must have been Floss. That was thoughtful. But no, I'm still pissed off at her. And at Hester. Even though she was nice enough to bathe me. I bat at my head with my hand. Arrrrgh. This fucking buzzing ...

When I'm dressed in a French Connection T-shirt and low-rise skinny jeans, the thought of going out into the lounge and facing everyone after my wailing and fainting fit makes me shudder. I hate showing weakness. I'm the strong one. The practical one. The one who's been keeping us fed via Elliott all these years. Maybe that's why Alexander targeted him because he knows he's the linchpin of the group? Take him, and we're forced out of hiding and into the streets, looking for food. And easier to pick off one by one.

But Alexander had the chance to kill me tonight, and he didn't. The curious look on his face when he tasted Elliott's blood and his remark 'How intriguing' give me the barest smidgeon of hope that my thrall is still alive and kicking. It's then that I realise what the buzzing in my head is. I let out a cry of stunned relief.

Now I know I'm going to need everyone's help, and it's that which forces me to head to the lounge. Everyone looks up as I walk in, jaw clenched. Floss and Damian are holding hands on the couch. He's white-faced and nervous. No surprise there. I notice he's wearing a spare pair of Elliott's jeans and his old Duran Duran T-shirt they've found in my wardrobe. Motherfucker. Elliott loves that T-shirt. It's even signed by the band. I grind my teeth. But Hester gestures to my chair, which has a mug of blood in front of it. I give her a stiff nod and take a seat.

No one says anything as I take a long swallow of warm blood. It slips down my throat and warms the cockles of my long-dead heart. A heart that, I'm afraid, has been compromised many years ago, and I haven't admitted to it.

Somewhat revitalised by the blood and feeling less inclined to scratch Damian's eyes out, I lean back in my chair and cross my legs.

'Right. Listen up, bitches. Elliott's alive, and we're going to rescue him.'

CHAPTER 3

I'm used to running around like a headless chicken on concert night, but this gig at the Royal Highland Exhibition Hall has been particularly stressful.

First, Andy kept breaking guitar strings at the soundcheck this afternoon, and the guys ribbed him about having sausage fingers. He's sensitive about his hands, so he got in a tizz and stormed offstage. Then when he'd been hugged by everyone and apologised to, they continued. But Simon had been nursing a sore throat since Manchester, so his voice sounded pretty rough. He decided to power through and gargle Epsom salts before the show, so I had to source a bag and get it sent to his hotel room. A couple of speakers blew for no reason, and then Nick's synthesiser wasn't triggering properly, which took ages for the keyboard tech to sort out. It seemed to be one thing after the other.

And this weather wasn't helping things. It was pissing

with rain when we arrived tonight and colder than a witch's tit. God knows why we had to come to Edinburgh in December. Sure, the Scots want to see Duran Duran play live (who wouldn't?). But there's been no thought for us lackeys who have to sprint around outside, doing various jobs. By the time I'd finished, my nuts were practically frozen.

Don't get me wrong. As a roadie for the most famous band on earth right now, I love my job and wouldn't change it for the world. But I'm still jet-lagged from Australia, where the Sing Blue Silver Tour started in November. So far, they've played eleven concerts in five weeks, and this is just the beginning. A gruelling schedule of concert dates is planned throughout December up until Christmas. Then we'll be in Japan and USA until April next year. Which is fine. It's what I signed up for. But part of the issue I'm having is that a few of the security team quit as they couldn't hack it. So I'm helping out their crew too, and I completely understand what they're dealing with.

Trying to keep the band protected from these fans is a nightmare. The boys can't even relax backstage after a concert because these women are fucking feral and storm the corridors, looking for them. They want them to sign their tits. They want their sweaty towels. They want the water bottles that they've sucked from. Want, want, want.

Most of them we manage to herd off at the pass, but a few do escape through. The uproar from those who don't makes my hair stand on end and my dick shrivel. I've even taken it on the chin a few times when they've lashed out in their distress. I imagine this is what it was like for the Beatles: the screaming, the crying, the fainting ... the punching.

Thankfully, the band is playing their final set now. Two more songs to go: 'Rio' and then 'Girls on Film'. Then they'll make a run for it out the back way. No hanging around tonight. They're heading straight to the hotel on their tour bus. We're off to Leeds tomorrow, and it's going to be an early start, so there'll be no partying for the band or crew. Everyone needs to arrive without hangovers for the afternoon soundcheck at Queens Hall.

I'll join them after I've tidied up. Their dressing room looks like a bomb has gone off in here with all their outfits, towels, and discarded water bottles. I consider hoarding a few and making some money off of their lip imprints, but in the end, I bundle them all into a black rubbish bag for the cleaners in the morning.

By the time I've finished, my eyes are drooping, and I'm looking forward to my bed. The thought makes me laugh a little. What am I, 23 going on 83? When I leave the dressing room, I'm not expecting to see a wall of hormonal women in the corridor as the security has been tighter here. But there are still twenty or so hanging around.

A ripple of anticipation goes through them when they spot me in my leather jacket with teased-up blond hair sauntering towards them. But then someone calls out, 'It's nae Simon! It's nae even Nick!' There's a rumble of despondent groans.

I get this a lot because I dress like Simon does. And I don't want to blow my own trumpet here, but I've been told I'm as good-looking as he is. I'm not his height of six feet two, but near enough at five foot eleven. But that doesn't make a difference to the fans. I'm not him. Usually, it's a minor irritation, and I brush it off. But tonight I'm tetchy because I'm tired, and these Duran Duran fans are soooo demanding.

Strolling up to them, I say in a loud voice, 'You're wasting your time hanging around, ladies. I'm their roadie, and the band isn't here. They left an hour ago. So you might as well go home.'

'I don't believe you. They always hang out backstage after concerts and meet their fans.' A blonde girl at the front of the group puts her hands on her hips and scowls at me. She's eye-catchingly pretty with scarlet lips and shaggy blonde hair à la Bonnie Tyler. She has a raspy voice like hers too. I can't help staring at her, taking in the sparkly tight green top, short black skirt, and spike-heeled leather boots wrapped around long slender calves. The other women throw me dark looks and mutter.

'Yeah, I bet he's lying.'

'Let us meet them.'

'We paid good money for our tickets.'

'We've been waiting to see them.'

It's not at all what I want to say. What I want to say is 'Better luck next time, ladies.' But somehow, I find myself opening my mouth, and this falls out: 'Come on then. But just you.'

I point at the blonde girl, and she smiles at me all sugary sweet now. 'That's more like it,' she says.

There's swearing and colourful cursing, as well as kicking and pounding of walls behind us, but the blonde girl pays them no heed. I take it no one here is her particular friend.

'What's your name?' I ask her as we walk towards the dressing room door.

'Sadie,' she says huskily, and a shiver rolls down my spine.

'So you want to meet Simon, I take it?'

'Yes,' she says decisively. 'Simon.'

'What about John? He's pretty popular with the ladies.'

'He's OK. But Simon's my favourite.'

I drag my hand over my face. Why the hell I'm taking her

to an empty dressing room, I don't know. But then I decide that she's been so bolshy, it serves her right to see that I was telling the truth.

I open the door and stand back. 'After you.'

She grins at me, and lust spears my groin. Wowser, as they say in Australia, she really is stunning! I'm actually glad that Simon isn't here as I'd be green-eyed with jealousy if he decided to hook up with her. Sadie shakes her hair back and straightens her spine, preparing to meet her idol. She steps into the empty room; and I watch her, leaning against the doorframe, my eyes raking over her long legs and sexy black leather boots.

Sadie swivels round, her lips pressed into a flat line. 'Where is he?'

I smirk. 'Maybe he's in the toilet, taking a dump.'

Her forehead wrinkles; and I feel an insistent pressing in the space between my eyebrows, like I got a headache coming on, which isn't surprising after the day I've had.

I sigh. 'I told you. They've left already.' I gesture to the soiled towels that I've herded into the middle of the room. 'But help yourself to a sweaty towel, though I'm not sure which one is Simon's. They've all got foundation on them.'

The girl's red lips part slightly, as if she's not used to someone getting the better of her. She's a bit of a spoiled madam, I conclude. But she also looks so disappointed that

I soften ... and go to my duffel bag and hand her one of my concert tour T-shirts.

'Look, here you go. Have this. It's signed by them and everything.'

Sadie takes it mutely. Without even a thank you. Oh well, I tried. If she's going to take it that badly ... I shake my head and say, 'Sorry, but at least you got to stand in their dressing room, which is more than some fans get to do. And you've got a signed T-shirt, which is gold.'

She still doesn't say anything, but the scowl is back. So I shrug and say, 'See ya', and walk off down the corridor, leaving her standing there, looking like she's going to blow a gasket. I snigger to myself, thinking, *She's even prettier when she's angry*. It's a pity I'm not supposed to get involved with fans as I would have totally invited her back to my hotel room. But I signed a contract stating that I would behave in a professional manner at all times when on tour.

OK, perhaps what just happened wasn't that professional of me, but Sadie kind of deserved it. *Sadie*. It's an unusual name; it reminds me a little of Salem and witches.

The rain has eased off as I step outside to the private parking lot, but the wind blows in cold gusts around my ears. Drawing my jacket around me tightly, I walk to the van and unlock the back door. I should check that there are some spare guitar strings for tomorrow since Andy went through so many today.

I'm rootling through a box of gear when there's a noise behind me. Then someone grabs the back of my jacket, and I'm picked up and thrown onto the van floor. My head knocks against an amplifier, and I lie there, dazed. The van door slams shut and locks, and footsteps crunch around the side. *Oh fuck*, I think. *This isn't good.*

The driver's door opens, and someone slithers into the leather seat. But from my position on the floor, I can't see who it is. But I'm not a lightweight guy, and the fact I've been picked up as if I were made of marshmallow and thrown in here suggests I'm dealing with a strong man.

The van starts up and starts backing out onto the road. Strangely, 'Total Eclipse of the Heart' by Bonnie Tyler is playing on the radio as we pull out onto the main road. My heart is pounding, and my hands start sweating as Bonnie warbles away about getting 'a little bit terrified'.

'W-where are you taking me?' I stutter fearfully.

A throaty female voice answers flatly from the driver's seat, 'To my place. You're going to pay for that little trick.'

CHAPTER 4

Sadie | Edinburgh, 1983

Slamming my foot on the accelerator, I roar off down the main road back to Edinburgh. I probably shouldn't be driving in a red mist of rage, but this guy has pissed me off to the point that I'm not thinking straight. How dare he trick me like that! And then laugh at me! I'm determined to wipe that smile off his face.

Even more annoying is that I can't read his mind. It's a buzzing blank of static. Like he has nothing but white noise between his ears. At any other time, I'd be intrigued. But right now, it's adding to my frustrated fury.

Roused from his fog of fear at being abducted, the guy yells, 'Pull over, you crazy woman!' There's a jolt on the back of my seat as he tries to crawl into the front. Attempting to stop a vampire driving a moving vehicle? That's brave and kind of stupid. He's going to get himself killed. I glance in the rear-view mirror and see his set jaw and determined expression.

'What the fuck are you doing?' he shouts right in my ear, and I flinch.

'Teaching you a lesson in manners,' I say calmly and slam my foot on the brake, so he shoots back with a yelp. *Hmm, he's going to hurt himself if he tries that again.* There's nothing for it. I bind him to the floor, so he's safe until I can get him home and do unsafe things to him. He calls me names and struggles, and I smirk to myself.

Of course, I have no fixed plan for what I'm going to do when I get him back to the flat. I'm getting more impulsive, not less, in my old age. When you're at the top of the food chain, you can get a little overconfident.

But it definitely feels good to use my powers again. I've had to keep them under wraps as I've been dating a human for the last six months. I'm now realising I've made a big mistake in doing that.

Typically, my flatmates and I don't date humans, because as vampires, we need to keep a low profile. But sometimes you meet a man who makes you want to bend the rules. Tim Rhodes is that man. A couple of months ago, he moved into the top floor of our New Town tenement. It was a surprise to get an invite to a flat-warming party he was throwing for the neighbours.

Floss instantly pushed for us to go. Hester was less sure about it and thought it was wiser to stay home. I couldn't have cared less. In the end, Floss twisted my arm, and Tim made a beeline for me as soon as we arrived. That night, we fell into bed and fell into a sort of relationship in the weeks after. I'm not sure how it even happened. But it's probably because he's handsome, charming, and a smart dresser. He owns a lot of tailored suits because he does something in finance. I forget what.

Anyway, I need to break up with him. It's not because he suspects that there's something strange about me, but more due to the fact that I read his mind the other night and discovered he wants to propose! He thinks he's in love with me, but he's not. He doesn't even know me. If he's expecting me to be his dutiful little wifey and give him children, he's in for a big shock. So yes, I need to break up with him, but I haven't found the right time to do it. It will be soon.

There's muttering and cursing from the van floor behind me, and I grin. This guy is high-spirited, cute, and he knows Simon Le Bon. So that makes him extremely appealing. I'm not going to hurt him. I might just scare him a little. So he tells me which hotel the band is staying in ...

CHAPTER 5

Sadie | Edinburgh, present day

Hester and Floss stare at me blankly when I tell them that Elliott is alive and we're going to rescue him. Or maybe it's because I called them 'bitches'. It's a figure of speech. They'll get over it. Damian just looks blank because he doesn't get anything. He's a liability.

'So let me get this straight,' says Hester. 'You want us to go on a wild goose chase based on the fact that you've heard *buzzing*?'

'The buzzing is Elliott trying to contact me,' I explain through gritted teeth. 'He's letting me know he's alive.'

'How come you can't talk to each other telepathically?' asks Damian, sounding interested. Do I deign to reply to him? Floss is giving me the evils, so I'd better. I need her help as she's the one with the blood bond with Alexander. And for moral support, since we've been friends for over a century. I trust her like a sister, though I probably don't give that impression. I know I've been acting cold and heartless to her about Damian, but it's only because I don't want to see her get hurt. And as far as I know, he hasn't agreed to being turned yet. He's liable to fuck off and leave her like men do in my experience. I've always had a niggling fear that if I hadn't compelled Elliott to do my bidding for all these years, he would have left me long ago.

I shrug. 'I don't know. It's always been that way with us. I can compel him, but I can't read his mind or project my thoughts to him. But at least we know Alexander's keeping him alive. For now.'

'What about trying hypnosis?' suggests Damian. 'I know it sounds a bit woo-woo, but with your heightened perceptions, you might be able to pick up on something. I did a self-hypnosis course last year to help with my anxiety, so I'm happy to put you under and supervise. It's quite safe.'

'That's a great idea!' says Floss, looking at him fondly. 'You're so clever.' She squeezes his arm, and he gives her a quick kiss on the lips.

I'm annoyed at them having a PDA in front of me when I'm obviously distressed, but I have no better ideas. 'OK, Doctor, you're on. But I'm warning you, my mind is difficult to control when it comes to the power of suggestion.'

I tip the mug to my lips and swallow the rest of the blood to bolster my strength. And to satiate my appetite so I don't accidentally bite him when I'm unconscious.

***

'Listen to my voice,' intones Damian. 'Your eyelids are starting to feel heavier.'

I crack open an eye from where I'm lying on the couch and look at him sitting beside me. 'Seriously?'

'Just try it, Sadie,' pleads Floss, hovering behind him. 'Do you want Elliott back or not?'

I snap my eye shut and try to relax, but my nerves feel like wire bands criss-crossing my body. But as he continues talking to me in a bland monotone, my fists unclench, and my shoulders lower from around my ears.

'Good, Sadie, very good,' Damian murmurs soothingly. 'Allow yourself to yield, just for a bit, and think of Elliott. His face, his smell, his jokes ...'

A smile flits across my lips. He's so funny, and he smells so good. 'Imagine that he's here with you now, and he's holding your hand.'

My eyelids flutter, and my fingers curl instinctively. Elliott's hands are warm and strong.

'Now I'm going to count backwards from ten, and with each number, you'll feel even more relaxed. Ten, nine ... Sinking deeper ... eight, seven ...'

At that point, I seem to drift off. Then I hear Damian's voice loud and clear. 'How are you, Sadie?'

'Good,' I mumble.

'What do you feel?'

'A slight rocking motion.'

'Excellent. Can you see anything?'

'No, it's … it's cramped and dark. And there's something pressing against my face.' I stiffen slightly.

'That's OK, just relax. You're safe and in control.' Damian's deep voice infiltrates the space. 'Tell me what you can hear.'

'A muffled thumping noise. It sounds like a drumbeat. Now there's talking, like a radio announcer.'

'Good, that's very good, Sadie. Can you hear what they're saying? Try and focus.'

I struggle to hear. 'No, it's too muffed. But—' Two words suddenly jump out at me clearly: 'Tay FM'.

When I open my eyes, Damian is smiling at me, and Hester and Floss are excitedly scrolling on their iPhones.

'What happened? Did it work?'

'I think you managed to connect with Elliott—' begins Damian.

Hester interrupts excitedly. 'You heard Alexander listening to Tay FM in the car. It's a local Perth radio station, so he must be up that way. He's driving north, to the Highlands.'

'That motherfucker!' I growl. 'If he touches a hair on Elliott's head, he'll have me to answer to.'

Chapter 6

Sadie | London, 1758

The gentleman's house is more than a five-minute stroll, and as we walk down one damp cobblestone street after another, I'm growing tired. It's been an eventful night, and I've decided that I've been too hasty in agreeing to go with him. I would rather be at the pub having a drink with the girls, then heading home to bed.

'How much farther?' I ask impatiently, glancing up at him.

We've kept to the darkened back alleys. But under the occasional street lamp, I've glimpsed the tip of a nose and a flash of a dimpled chin and felt the strong grip of his leather-gloved hand tightening round mine whenever I stumbled. But now as we emerge into a wider road with better lighting, his profile is outlined in stark relief as he glances left and then right up the empty street. I catch my breath. I have been walking with a beautiful man. A man who has been sculpted from pale marble by some master creator; his features are elegant and strong, and he stands taller than average, black curls tumbling unbidden to the upturned collar of his dark woollen cloak. Beneath its swinging folds is the merest glimpse of a red silk waistcoat. I've had some handsome customers in my time, but none who made my cunny slick with desire from a single glance. I'm tempted to forgo my payment and fuck him for the sheer pleasure of it. And it would be a pleasure, I've no doubt.

The gentleman looks down at me, his striking amber eyes flashing with heat, as if he can read my lustful thoughts. He tightens his hand in mine, and his soft sensual lips curve in a smile.

'My house is right here. I apologise for the roundabout route. There are some people I wish to avoid.' His voice is smooth and deep, authoritative, and carries a hint of confidentiality like he's trusting me with a secret.

He doesn't elaborate further. But I know, from that remark, that he's not an upstanding member of society. He's evading detection for some reason. Just as I am.

'I understand,' I tell him with a light touch to my nose. 'Your secrets are safe with me, as I hope mine are with you.'

'Good. And yes, do not fear. Discretion is my middle name.'

What is his name? I wonder. But he may not want to tell me if he's that keen on hiding.

The gentleman releases my hand and places his on the small of my back. He guides me towards a dark-green door across the street. The place looks right posh with a neatly tended front garden and a gravel pathway. There's even a black iron gate, which he unlocks and swings open for me to enter.

'After you, Miss Smith.'

That makes me hesitate in surprise. 'But ... how do you know my name?'

He cocks his head. 'I have eyes and ears. You're quite famous in certain circles.'

I smile a little. *Even royal ones.* 'Oh. I suppose I am.'

'Shall we go in?'

I take a step forward. But something about the way he's standing there as still as a statue, amber eyes unblinking, makes me hesitate.

'Come now. The night isn't getting any younger, and neither are we. I hear you're a girl who likes to have fun, and I promise it will be an experience to remember.' He places a gloved hand softly on my cheek, and I smell expensive leather and the sweet trace of roses. He must have some planted in the garden. But why on earth am I dithering out here when I could be inside with him? I smile, feeling a little dazzled, and walk without a worry or a care through the gate.

CHAPTER 7

Elliott | Edinburgh, 1983

The van is careening all over the road. Whoever Sadie is, she needs to enrol in a driver education programme. I'm tempted to call out some disparaging remarks about women drivers, but I think it will piss her off even further.

But I can't stop her either as, weirdly, my limbs are pinned to the floor in the back of the van, so I can't move. On one hand, it's a good thing. I'm not being flung against the walls every time she makes a sharp turn. But also very bad as I'm worried that she's injected me with some kind of drug to make my body heavy. I'm not sure what that would be, but I'm starting to realise I've made a huge mistake in inviting her to the dressing room at all (though I was surprised to hear the words coming out of my mouth!). One of the clauses in my contract specifically says not to interact with fans as they may be temporarily insane and that I should keep my distance wherever possible.

It's the logical explanation to what's going on: Sadie is a deranged Duran Duran fan, and she's kidnapped me. All I can do is stay alert and grab something to use as a weapon when we stop. Because I'm not sure what she's going to do when she gets me to her place, and that scares the bejesus out of me.

After a while, the van jerks to a stop, and I assume we're now in the city centre. A car swooshes past on the wet street, and yellow light spills into the back of the van through the windscreen. Sadie gets out, and her high heels tip-tap to the back door. I test my hands, and they come free off the floor, and my legs can move now too. The drug must have worn off! I have seconds to spare.

Quickly, I crawl on my hands and knees to the box of guitar gear that I was looking through earlier before all this happened. I know for certain that there's a tuning fork in there. I wish I had a goddamn Uzi to scare the life out of this woman, but me wielding a tuning fork will hopefully make her back off. Yes! I was right. I crouch in readiness, gripping the tuning fork tightly. When the door swings open to reveal Sadie, she stares at me in surprise, as if she wasn't expecting me to be armed. *That's right you, nutter. I'm not going down without a fight!*

A cold waft of winter air rushes over my neck, and I shiver. I wield the tuning fork like a tiny sword in front of me and say in a low menacing tone, 'Back away from the van, and I won't hurt you.'

Sadie's eyes drop to the tuning fork, and she smirks. 'What are you going to do with that? Make sure I'm playing at the right pitch?'

She takes a step forward, and I stab viciously at the air. 'I mean it.'

'I'm sure you do, Elliott Blythe,' she says in a smooth unconcerned tone. 'But resistance is futile. You're coming with me, whether you like it or not.'

Before I can ask how the hell she knows my name, the tuning fork drops out of my hand and clatters harmlessly to the van floor. My legs hop down from the van, and I start lurching towards one of the doors in the tenement flats we're parked next to. *What are you doing, legs?* Going into Sadie's flat wasn't the plan. It's the last thing I want to do! But I can't seem to stop and make myself run away. It's like my legs are possessed by some unseen force.

The van door slams behind me. Then a finger pokes me between the shoulder blades.

'Keep walking. Luckily for you, we live in a basement flat, not the top floor.'

I moan softly in terror. The word 'basement' sounds ominous. And who's 'we'? Am I about to encounter more wacko Duran Duran fans?

Feeling like I'm in a nightmare, my legs descend the short flight of steps to an overgrown courtyard and then underneath an archway. However, I'm slightly too tall to fit under it easily, and the top of my head scrapes against the edge. I whine in pain.

'Whoops, sorry about that,' says Sadie lightly behind me. 'Forgot to make you duck.'

What the hell does that mean? I wonder. *Is Sadie controlling me? But how?* Unease skitters down my spine. I'm starting to think that she's something other than a loopy fan. Something much worse.

'Knock on the door,' demands Sadie, and despite trying with all my might not to, my hand lifts and raps the lion's head door knocker.

It opens, and a pretty young woman with short punkish hair looks back at me. She's around my height, wearing ripped jeans and a black T-shirt and looks a bit like the lead singer from Siouxsie and the Banshees. Her pale skin and big violet eyes seem to glow, but there are no lights on in the flat behind her. We're standing in darkness.

'Hello. Who are you?' she asks curiously.

I open my mouth to speak, but nothing comes out.

'He's with me' comes Sadie's voice from behind my left shoulder.

My body jerks forward, and it's like I'm being urged to

step into the flat by unseen hands. *No*, I think. *I will not go in there*. But the force is too strong; and I stumble forward, past the surprised woman, and go for a small slide along the entryway rug. It smells sweet in here, like someone's gone to town with the floral air freshener. My pulse elevates. *Is it to cover the smell of dead bodies?*

Whispering ensues behind me, and I stand stock-still (not that I have any other choice) and listen intently. What they say may be important for figuring out what on earth's going to happen to me. And also be used as evidence in court if I ever manage to escape. Which I'm determined to do.

But the brief snatch of conversation I hear between the two women only consists of: 'What the fuck, Sadie?' and 'Shh, listen'.

No other talking ensues, so I'm not sure how they're communicating. Sign language? This is getting weirder by the minute. And why are there no lights on? I suppose that is comforting in some respects as murdering someone in the dark might be quite difficult.

CHAPTER 8

Sadie | Edinburgh, 1983

My intention had been to try and force Elliott Blythe to tell me where the band was staying so I could hang outside the hotel and meet Simon when they surfaced. I found the guy's name badge on the dashboard with his smug grinning photo on it, as if to say 'Look at me. I know Duran Duran'. Grrrr, it's so fucking annoying I can't read his mind. It would make things a lot easier. But he's resistant to any mind probing. And I was concentrating hard! So much so that I was driving all over the road. However, as it proved difficult to compel him in any way but physically, I gave up on that idea. But then another one hit me like a slap of bat wings. Oooh yes, it was a much better idea, something that would suit me and my flatmates long-term.

This is how our situation currently stands: We can't keep feeding on random drunks and homeless people in the dead of night and memory-wiping them. Some bystander or curtain twitcher is going to notice sooner or later and report us. Then the police will be involved, and I don't particularly want to memory-wipe an entire division.

No, we need someone who can get us blood on a regular basis. Hester worked at a blood donation centre for a year and managed to sneak some out before she was fired for reasons unknown. It could have been because her phlebotomy skills were shit (she's precise when biting for blood, not so much drawing it with a syringe). No matter. I've been considering running an underground blood donation service for years. And now Elliott's dropped into my lap. He's the perfect person to manage it for us. He may need some coercing ... I mean *convincing*. But I'm sure I can find a way to do that. I saw the way he was ogling me. I'm sure after a little vampiric seduction, I'll have him eating out of the palm of my hand. Or eating something else ... Whoops, I'd better concentrate on driving rather than seducing Elliott. I nearly hit a postbox then!

* * *

When we arrive, Elliott turns feisty and tries to stab me with a tuning fork, which makes me want to laugh. I put a stop to that nonsense and compel him to walk into our flat, which he does with some resistance. This guy is intriguing me with his determination to fight my powers. Who does he think he is?

Floss is understandably confused at the whole business. 'What the fuck, Sadie?' she says, staring at Elliott, who's sliding around on the rug.

Dammit, I'll have to fill her in mentally. Floss can fly. However, her telepathic skills are limited. But I can project my thoughts to her and pick up on what she's thinking. 'Shh, listen.'

Me: *I know this looks odd, but there's a method to my madness.*

Floss: *You kidnapped a guy! I knew I should have gone with you to that concert. I had a feeling you were going to try and meet Simon Le Bon. But this isn't him? I mean, he's cute and all, but—*

Me: No, *he's not, more's the pity. He's Duran Duran's roadie ... It's a long story. I'll fill you in later. Anyway, now that he's here, I thought he could be of use to us.*

Floss: *Oh? We'd better get Hester in on this. She's in the lounge, reading.*

Me: *OK, I'll move him in there.*

Floss: *He looks really annoyed ... and tired. Are you sure you should have—*

Me: *I'm handling it!*

But she is right. Elliott's shoulders are slumping with

exhaustion. I forget that these fragile humans need seven hours of shut-eye a night.

Me: *Change of plan. I'll put him in my bed so he can sleep. I'll meet you in the lounge shortly.*

Floss raises her eyebrows briefly but doesn't argue. She glides off to the lounge in the darkness. Elliott doesn't see her feet aren't touching the floor because his eyes aren't attuned to the darkness. But I march him off to my bedroom quickly anyway. He's going to find out very soon who he's dealing with and why he shouldn't have played that joke on me.

Once we're in my bedroom, I whisk him over to the bed, flop him down on his back, spreadeagle him, and mentally hold his arms and legs in place. He immediately struggles and tries to wrench his wrists away from the invisible bonds. But that's not going to happen. I've been perfecting my technique since 1758, and no man has ever escaped.

He moves his mouth, but nothing comes out but a thin whimper. Oh yeah, I forgot I compelled him to remain quiet in the van. I let him speak, curious to hear what he has to say.

'I won't go to the police, I promise. Please let me go.'

His tone is low and urgent, his eyes wide with fear. And his heart is pumping wildly. The smell of his blood permeates the room; and suddenly, I'm on high alert, feeling my fangs extend. I lick my lips and circle the bed. The room is dark enough that he can't see me, but he can hear the tap of my heels, and his head swings in the direction of my footsteps.

'Nothing's going to happen to you,' I say in a velvety voice. 'Just go to sleep. There's a good boy.'

He whimpers again. So I send him some calming energy; and in a few minutes, his muscles slacken, and his eyes close. *There we go. No harm done.* I swallow, pushing aside the need to feed, which is clouding my senses. I could take a drink. But for some reason, I'm holding back, partly out of loyalty to Tim upstairs. I drink from him on occasion when he's asleep when I can't be bothered going out hunting with Floss and Hester. And drinking from Elliott feels like I'd be cheating on Tim, though he has no idea I do it—I suction discreetly from his glutes, where he can't see the marks. But I can't keep doing that. It's another reason why I need to break it off (as if him thinking of proposing wasn't enough!).

While Elliott sleeps, I sit on the bed next to him and gently brush back his teased golden hair, admiring his handsome face. He's not Simon, but he is still a good-looking guy. I trail my hand down his broad chest, looking at the white Duran Duran concert T-shirt he's wearing. It's different from the one he gave me. It's also white, but it has a map on it. This one has a tiger's eye on the front surrounded by red and blue spikes and various symbols, including a crescent moon. I trace the outline of the moon, and Elliott's nipples rise in little peaks under the material. *Hmm, interesting.* My hand hovers, but I don't touch them. My hand moves lower, over his stomach, feeling the hard spring of his ab muscles. I gently pull his T-shirt out of his jeans, lift it up to his ribs, and gaze at his six-pack. *Mmm, he's got a great body too.* I run my fingers lightly over his skin, and gooseflesh appears. *Hah, he likes that.* A quick glance at his crotch and I see his jeans have started bulging too. I shift on the bedcover. Elliott's sleep erection is making me wet between the legs. I contemplate unbuttoning his Levi's 501s ... just for a little peek ...

Hester's voice appears in my mind before I can block her. I do most of the time, but sometimes she slips in when I'm distracted. Like now.

Sadie, what are you doing? Floss said you've kidnapped someone! We need to talk about this. Lounge now!

I sigh and tuck Elliott's T-shirt back in neatly and give his rising and falling stomach a little pat.

Be there in two ticks.

CHAPTER 9

Sadie | Edinburgh, present day

After my hypnosis session, I'm surprisingly clear-headed about the next steps.

'We're going to have to track Alexander to the Highlands. You,' I say sharply pointing at Damian. 'Can you drive?'

He nods. 'Yeeess. But I don't have a car.'

'Can you get one?'

Damian thinks for a minute. 'I could borrow my dad's. He doesn't use it much since he works from home, and it should fit all of us.'

'Great. Let's get ready.'

He blinks at me. 'Uh, now? It's after midnight. My dad will be asleep. Besides, I can't take off up to the Highlands. I have patients tomorrow.'

Floss rubs his arm. 'He needs to sleep too.'

I roll my eyes. These bloody humans with their jobs and needing sleep. Floss should have turned Damian rather than wiffle-waffling around with him. Frustrated at the entire lack of urgency, I get up and start pacing. Grrrr, this is all taking way too long. I feel like running outside right now and stealing a car. But I've never bothered getting a licence, and though I can drive, I'm not that good at it. In my highly emotional state, I'm liable to crash. If only Elliott still had his van, Damian could drive that, but he sold it years ago.

'Fine. You can sleep for a few hours. But we need to go after that. As for your patients—'

'I could say I've had a family emergency and will be away for a few days ... I'll get Maggie, my receptionist, to reschedule them,' says Damian quickly.

'Good.'

'Should we book a hotel somewhere?' suggests Hester, looking at me. 'We'll need a pit stop. And we should probably take the rest of the blood bags to keep our strength up. Unless you want to stop at towns on the way?'

I glance at Damian, and he goes a bit pale, as if he's realised he's going to be chauffeuring a car full of bloodsucking vampires.

'We'll definitely take the blood, then see how things pan out,' I say. 'It all depends where Alexander's taking him. I don't particularly want to have to resort to hunting after all these years, but we might have to if we need to ... refuel.' I lick my lips and stare at Damian's neck.

Floss jumps up and shuffles him out of the room and down to her lair. I laugh a little when I pick up on her indignation.

Hands off—no one's going to be biting Damian but me!

Hester accompanies me to my bedroom, then disappears to hers, and I manage to get a couple of hours' sleep. Then I jerk awake, thinking Elliott is lying beside me and realise with a sinking feeling that it's just an empty space. Even though he has his own flat, he sleeps over on a regular basis, not that we do much sleeping. I miss him. A lot. It's hard for me to admit that, but I do. I wouldn't be undertaking this mission to the Highlands and risking my own neck if I didn't.

I check in with Floss telepathically to try and get her to wake Damian up, but she says he's exhausted and to quit it. She's getting quite feisty and protective now that she's got a boyfriend and getting some regular action. He must be good in bed if she's so enamoured with him.

I bet he's not as good as Elliott, though. He knows exactly what I like. I close my eyes and try to not to think about the worst-case scenario. I haven't heard the buzzing noise for a while, but that could mean he's sleeping. Or already dead.

By the time we set off, it's approaching 7 a.m., and I've been packed and ready to go for hours. We each have a small tote with a change of clothes and toiletries, as well as a cooler for the blood bags. Thanks to Elliott bringing round a fresh supply yesterday, we have about ten, which should be enough to keep us going. I assume we're going to catch the bus to Blackford to collect the car, but Floss says no. That we have to stop off at Damian's first so he can get changed and pack some clothes in a backpack as he feels weird wearing Elliott's stuff. We all have to go as he's nervous since Alexander was near the flat last night. I roll my eyes and am tempted to say that by this time, Alexander is deep in the Highlands and undoubtedly snacking on Elliott. But I don't say anything.

I need the support of the coven, and Damian's hypnosis skills, if I want to have any chance of rescuing Elliott. So I will be nice Sadie, patient Sadie. Even if I feel like I want to rip everyone's heads off for being so goddamn slow!

Damian's dad—or Malcolm, I remember him being called— is surprised to see us all on his doorstep this early in the morning.

His eyes rest on Damian, who's holding hands with Floss, and they have a short conversation about borrowing the car. Hester and I stand a few steps back, and I play with a leaf on a shrub, not wanting him to recognise me.

But after he invites us in and I slide my sunglasses to the top of my head, I can't avoid his curious gaze. Floss told me about the photo of us at Tim's flat-warming party and that Damian's dad remembered my name, so he definitely knows who I am. Awkward.

We stand around in the kitchen while Malcolm puts the kettle on. 'Does anyone want a tea or coffee?' We all shake our heads.

'So you're off up north?' he asks Damian, deliberately ignoring us girls. His fingers are quivering as he adds a teabag to his cup. Yeah, he knows we're not normal, but he's trying to hide it well for Damian's sake. Tim might have said something to him about me as well when we broke up.

'Yes, it's a spur of the moment thing. I had some leave owing, and we decided to go last night.'

'Are you OK with driving?'

Damian shrugs. 'I think so.'

Floss squeezes his hand. Oh yeah, he was involved in a car accident a few years ago, wasn't he? That's nice of him to offer. Then again, I kind of forced him into it.

Malcolm leans against the counter, sipping his tea. I'm so tempted to read his mind to find out what he's thinking, but part of me doesn't want to know. I dumped his brother in a cold-hearted manner, so he's not going to be thinking anything nice.

But then he takes a deep breath and says, 'How are you, Sadie? Long time no see.' OK, it looks like he's going to avoid the elephant in the room: *Why do you still look the same as you did in 1983?*

I give him a brief nod. 'Good, thanks, Malcolm. How's Tim?' I ask the question out of politeness but then instantly regret it when Malcolm brightens.

'He's OK. Well, he was the last time I spoke to him. It's been a few months. He's off-grid, living near Pitlochry. If you're up that way, you should drop in. He'd love to see you.'

Is he joking? I say to Hester. *I really don't think he would. I dumped him like a hot potato. The guy was about to ask me to marry him!*

It's been ages. He's probably over it by now, she replies. *It's not a bad idea to look him up. Then we don't have to stay in a hotel.*

'We'll discuss it on the way,' says Damian nervously, seeing my jaw clench. 'We're not exactly sure where we're going yet.'

Malcolm chuckles, and the tension in the room eases. 'Sounds like the trips me and my friends used to take. I have a couple of tents you can use if you get stuck.'

I shudder. Camping. I abhor it. In any season. Even staying with an ex-boyfriend sounds better than that.

Malcolm pulls out a nearby drawer and chucks a set of keys at Damian, who catches them in one hand. 'There's a quarter of a tank, so you'll need to fill up on the way. Have fun.'

My lips stretch in the semblance of a smile. We're trying to rescue my thrall from a vengeful vampire. We may all die in the process.

'Yeah, should be good,' I say with a touch of sarcasm. 'I'm looking forward to it.'

Soon afterwards, we're on the road in a red Toyota Corolla: Damian behind the wheel, Floss next to him in the passenger seat, and Hester and me in the back. Hester has to bend her head slightly because she's so tall. I don't envy the crick in her neck she's going to have later on.

Damian's eyes meet mine in the rear-view mirror. 'Are you going to memory-wipe my dad?'

I arch an eyebrow. 'I'd have to memory-wipe him all the way back to 1983 as I get the feeling Tim may have said something to him at the time. He probably pushed it out of his mind as ludicrous, but meeting Floss and now me again has confirmed what Tim suspected.'

Floss swivels slightly in her seat to look at me. 'What would Tim have said?'

I shrug and stare out the window. 'Something along the

lines of me being a "stone-cold freak". That's what he said when we broke up. He was upset. It wasn't an amiable break-up.'

'So his stone-cold ex dropping in to see him forty years later might not be a good idea?' quips Damian. I know he's attempting to lighten the tense atmosphere, but it only serves to irritate me.

'You think?' I snap sarcastically.

No one says anything—for a very long time.

Damian is driving like an old man, and I'm ready to burst out my skin with frustration.

I can't help complaining to Floss: *Damian's slower than a grandpa. We got passed by a little old lady back there.*

Floss: *He's being cautious. After the accident.*

Me: *That was years ago. Tell him to put the pedal to the metal, for God's sake.*

Floss: *No, it will stress him out!*

With all the grunting and eyebrow fluttering going on, I'm sure Damian knows we're talking about his driving. His ears are red, and his hands are white-knuckled on the wheel.

Floss puts her hand on his leg and murmurs soothingly to him, 'You're doing great, babe. Just drive at the speed you feel comfortable at.'

I roll my eyes. *These two are too cutesy for words*, I

think to Hester. But she wisely stays out of it, head down, scrolling on her phone.

I'm aware that not having my morning dose of Elliott's blood is making me more of a bitch than usual. I missed his arms around me, feeding from his neck and chatting afterwards. All I've got now is the comforting buzz in my head that tells me he's alive. He's my glue, and without him, I can feel myself starting to become unstuck emotionally and mentally. I *have* to keep it together, for Elliott's sake.

Chapter 10

Elliott | Edinburgh, 1983

There's a dull ache in my shoulders, which my brain tells me is from the busy day I had yesterday setting up equipment for the band. But as I come to slowly, I realise I can't move my arms or my legs, and I'm not in my hotel room. I blink in the grey light filtering through the curtains. Where the hell am I? As I struggle to sit up and see what's restraining me, a slim hand with pearly pink nails is laid flat on my stomach.

'Lie still,' says a husky voice that sends a frisson of fear to my gut.

Chest tightening in alarm, slowly, I turn my head to meet a pair of arctic-blue eyes. Fuck, it's Sadie, the crazed fan from last night. She's lying stretched out next to me in a pink T-shirt and black skirt. Her head is propped on her hand, and she's surveying me coolly.

Panicked thoughts start flooding my brain. *Oh no, I'm still here at her flat! It wasn't a bad dream that she kidnapped me! Thank God my clothes are still on!*

Sadie gives me a carefree smile, as if it's completely normal to have kidnapped someone and tied them to their bed overnight. She lifts her hand from my stomach and waggles her fingers at me.

'Morning, sleepyhead.'

Declining to reply, I yank at the arm restraints. Twisting my head, I can see my wrists against the bedposts. There's nothing there, yet I'm held tight. How can that be? See-through plastic or something?

'What the hell are you doing?' I croak. 'Let me go. I've got to get to the hotel. We're driving to Leeds this morning.'

Sadie casually looks at her watch. 'It's coming up on nine. I think they've probably left without you by now.'

I blink at her. My brain is now starting to comprehend how fucked I am. No one knows I'm here.

'The band will tell the police I'm missing. I'm an important member of the crew ...' I gabble. 'They'll be out looking for me.'

'Hmm, will they, Elliott Blythe?' she purrs, raking her gaze down my chest. Something about her voice is seriously sexy, and I feel my dick stirring in my jeans, which shocks me. Surely, I'm not *attracted* to my kidnapper. That's mad. I've been kidnapped for one night, and already I've got Stockholm syndrome!

'I phoned your hotel first thing this morning and asked to speak to the band manager, Mick,' she continues. 'Gosh, was he grumpy! Certainly not a ray of sunshine at 7 a.m.'

'How do you know my name and where I'm staying?' I ask suspiciously.

She shrugs. 'Not hard. There was a name badge and a folder with your itinerary in the van. Anyway, back to Mick. He was even grumpier when I said you weren't going to be able to continue with the tour because you had a raging case of genital herpes. You were too ashamed to tell him yourself or face the band. So you'd caught a flight back to London last night and asked your mother to phone him.'

My mouth falls open. 'My mother!'

She hits my arm playfully and giggles. 'It wasn't your real mother, silly. It was me pretending to be her. You don't want your mother knowing something like that!'

I shake my head in confusion. 'So they're not looking for me?'

'No, but you'll get paid up until Christmas. He wasn't too happy about your behaviour.' She wags a finger at me and clicks her tongue. 'Naughty Elliott, you're not meant to sleep with the fans. Now you're on a course of antivirals.'

'But I didn't sleep with anyone!' I cry, yanking uselessly at the restraints. 'And I don't have herpes! You're a sick and twisted woman. You've cost me the best job of my life. I'm

Duran Duran's roadie, for fuck's sake.'

Sadie lifts an eyebrow. 'Not anymore, I'm afraid. Now you're working for us.'

While I'm gazing at her with my jaw slack, Sadie says the exact specifications of what this job entails will be explained to me after I've had a shower and some breakfast. Somehow, I'm released from the bed, and my legs march promptly into the bathroom. A clean towel is thrust at me, the door is closed and locked, and I'm left to my own devices. After checking that there's no window from which to escape, I sink onto the toilet seat and bury my head in my hands. Fuuuuuck, I'm in a big pickle.

But after a few minutes of wigging out, my pragmatic side kicks in. First, I don't think Sadie is going to murder me, which is a huge relief. Second, I think she's given me a strong drug that is making me more inclined to do what she says. Third, I've got the skills to cope with this exact situation.

There's a reason why I was hired to make sure Duran Duran's live concerts run smoothly: I can problem-solve and keep my cool under pressure, I'm physically strong, and I have excellent mental endurance.

All I have to do is go along with what she says for the moment, keep my wits about me, and wait for an opportunity to make a break for it. It shouldn't be too difficult. Easier than fixing a sound system failure mid-performance anyway.

Feeling a bit better now that I have a plan, I gulp some water from the bathroom tap, take a piss, and hop into the shower. All going well, I'll be out of here in a few hours and on the road to Leeds. The boys are going to laugh their heads off when they hear about this!

After I've washed and dressed in the same clothes I was wearing yesterday, I knock on the door. It opens immediately, but there's no one behind it, which is a bit strange. Before I have a chance to think, I'm propelled out of the bathroom. Despite me struggling to go left towards the front door (which I can see right there!), I'm forced right and into a comfortably furnished, but dimly lit lounge. It's a basement flat and winter, so there's not much daylight at all. I squint, and the main light switches on. Ah, that's better.

Now I can see a woman with red hair tied up in a ponytail lying on a cream couch. An open book is propped up on her knees. Sitting on the arm of the couch is the brunette who answered the door last night. They're both strikingly pretty, but my gaze lands on Sadie, who's leaning on the windowsill. Her small pink T-shirt is tight around her breasts, and I can tell she's not wearing a bra as her nipples are clearly defined. And her black skirt is more of a belt, showing off bare legs that resemble smooth ivory. They're crossed at the ankles, which taper into delicate arched feet with pink toes. I gulp, feeling that tug of attraction in my groin again. She's obviously insane, more's the pity, but she's super hot too.

Everyone is looking at me.

'Hi, Elliott,' Sadie drawls. 'How was your ... shower?'

Her sultry voice makes it sound like I was wanking off in there or something.

'Fine,' I say gruffly, determined not to blush in front of her. 'You mentioned something about breakfast?'

'As promised.' She nods to a side nook, where there's a table set with a plate and spoon, a box of cornflakes, a jug of milk, and a banana. Basic, but it's food, I guess. And it will help me think clearly and logically.

I shovel cereal into my mouth and chew rapidly, glancing at the two girls on the couch, who haven't spoken yet. But the brunette is staring at me curiously, as if she hasn't seen a man before. She seems a bit odd. And really pale, like she doesn't go outside much. The red-headed girl, with the long ponytail, is reading and acting like I don't exist.

'Hi, I'm Elliott. We met last night?' I address the brunette politely. Maybe if I get to know her, she can help me escape. She seemed shocked at seeing me at the front door.

The girl nods. 'We did. Nice to see you again.'

'Yes, sorry,' says Sadie. 'These are my flatmates, Floss and Hester.' She nods at each in turn. 'I've filled them in on the details, and we had a flat meeting about it last night. We all agree.' Her eyes slide to the redhead, whose lips are pursed. 'Well, Hester was a little resistant at first, but she's come round to my way of thinking. So the upshot is you're going to be staying here with us for a while. Until we get things set up anyway.'

I almost choke on my mouthful of half-chewed cereal. They're *all* fucking crazy! Then remember I need to stay cool and calm about this and obtain as much information as possible—for the police.

'Right,' I say. 'So are you going to tell me what this job is?'

Sadie gnaws at her bottom lip, and a flash of unease crosses her face. It's the first time I've seen her look rattled.

'It's ... er ... a humanitarian position.'

'Humanitarian? I don't get it.'

Sadie rolls her eyes. 'We need blood, OK? A regular supply. And you're going to get it for us.'

I blink, looking round at them. 'B-blood?' I stutter. Blood is not good. Blood equates to murder.

'Yes,' says Sadie impatiently. 'To drink.'

My physical reaction to this statement—namely heart

pounding and palms sweating—seems to be causing extreme interest amongst everyone. All three are now leaning forward slightly, noses raised, and their eyes are focused solely on my neck.

I think I'm in deep shit.

CHAPTER 11

Sadie | London, 1758

I'm escorted through a narrow hallway that leads to a large back bedroom. It's well furnished and has a feeling of snug comfort, especially when the gentleman lights the gas lamps and the room glows golden. I glance once at the big bed laid with a dark-green satin coverlet and then away, knowing that's where I'm to spend the rest of the evening.

Does he live here alone? I wonder, looking around at various items in the room. From the framed maps on the wall and the various knick-knacks—coloured glass bottles, jars of shells, carved animals—arranged haphazardly on the mantel, it appears he likes to travel, picking up various treasures here and there as he goes.

The gentleman removes his black woollen cloak with a flourish, hooking it onto a coat stand. Again, I'm struck by how breathtakingly handsome he is. He gives the impression of old money and ancient castles; of claret sipped by a fireside after a hearty meal.

'Am I permitted to know your name, sir?' I ask.

'Mr Darius Vexley,' he says gruffly. 'But please call me Darius for the duration of our appointment, Miss Smith.' His lips quirk. 'I enjoy hearing women call out my name in the throes of passion.'

He's confident, I think. I suppose I could fake it and moan his name if that's what he likes. Despite my popularity for making men spill their seed, I don't usually orgasm myself. Not that they care. They're paying me for their pleasure, not mine. I can't even remember the last time I came … I think it was last month with that duke fellow who insisted on several more goes until I did, but he never paid extra …

Darius points to a wooden changing screen with pretty yellow roses and green vines painted on the panels. 'You can get changed behind there. You'll find water, soap, and a robe for your use. Please wash thoroughly, especially between your legs. I want only the scent of lavender down there, not other men.'

He doesn't say it unkindly. Rather, he states it with no broach for argument. It's not an unreasonable request. I have been with several other men this evening, and I can smell stale sweat wafting from my armpits, thanks to the fright of the raid and our lengthy trek to his house.

'You might want to give me at least twenty minutes then. I'm a dirty girl.' I say it as a joke, hoping for a chuckle or a ribald comment.

But he doesn't smile, only gives a curt 'Very well, I'll be here when you emerge.'

So I dip my head and disappear behind the screen while he sits in an armchair and shakes out a newspaper. Hopefully, he's not going to be this serious in the sack. It's always better if the man has a sense of humour and we can have a laugh. Makes things less awkward too. I once had a man so shy that he refused to take his breeches off or look at me while he was performing. Just whipped out his long, thin dick, stuck it in me, and stared resolutely at the ceiling while he pumped away. I think he must've been religious or married as he kept muttering prayers under his breath. Thankfully, it was a one and done, and I haven't seen him since.

I hum a little ditty as I remove my dress and stays, throwing them over the top of the screen. The water in the jug is lukewarm when I dip my fingers in, and it occurs to me that it was boiled not long ago. That suggests Darius was prepared for me (or someone like me) to come back here with him ... He was out on the prowl. Uncertainty niggles at me, thanks to Mother Swift's warning. Is it wise to be here at his house? But the sooner I give him what he wants, the sooner I can get back home to bed for some shut-eye. And he looks and acts like a toff—he won't hurt me.

Shoving any doubtful thoughts to the back of my mind, I

soap the washcloth and scrub lavender-scented foam over my body, giving between my legs a good going-over. The rough cloth passing backwards and forwards over my cunny sparks desire. Yes, and I'm also curious to know what Darius has in store for me—too curious to listen to my common sense anyway.

I shrug into the green silk robe that has the same yellow roses embroidered on the lapels and emerge from behind the screen, glowing from my ablutions.

A corner of the newspaper lowers, and Darius slides an amber eye over me from top to toe. 'Come here,' he says. 'Over by the fire.'

In the time that I've been behind the screen, a cheerful fire has been built in the grate, flames now licking hungrily at the logs. The warmth is quickly eating into the chill of the room, and I'm happy to obey his request.

'Take off your robe,' Darius says in a low voice. 'I want to see you.' Again, there's that note of confidence and command, which reminds me that he's very in control of what happens. But I suppose he does hold the purse strings.

I undo the tie, and the silk robe slithers to the ground.

'Very nice,' he purrs, his gaze running over my full breasts, narrow waist, and flared hips. His eyes slide to my golden-curled cunny, and he licks his lips slowly, which makes my clit start pulsing.

'Turn around.'

With a smirk, I do so and sense his eyes raking over my behind, but without any heavy breathing, which usually ensues when men look at my pert bottom.

'Bend over and hold on to the mantel,' he says gruffly.

Surprised, I do as I'm told, presenting my bare arse to him.

The heat emanating from the fire warms my breasts and stomach to a rosy pink while I wait, not too sure what to expect since I'm usually instructed to 'lie on the bed and open my legs', not stand naked by the fireside.

Something ice-cold lightly touches the back of my upper thigh, and I jerk in shock.

'I apologise, Miss Smith. I have cold hands. So you may find my touch unpleasant to begin with.' Darius's voice hovers somewhere in the vicinity of my buttocks.

Is he on his knees?

'Call me Sadie,' I say, not sure if I like the thought of cold hands touching me. Warm and clammy is what I'm used to. 'Will you not warm your hands by the fire first?'

There's a pause.

'Thank you, Sadie. It will not help to do so.'

Cold hands it is then.

There's a press of frigid fingers on my hips, holding me steady, and I brace myself for a cock to enter me from behind—surely, that won't be cold! But something wholly unexpected occurs. A wet, frosty tongue begins lapping enthusiastically at my cunny entrance.

My fingers tighten on the mantel as it slithers and twirls around down there. Then it shifts to my clit, lapping and teasing. The combination of ice-cold licking below and shimmers of heat from the fire on my thighs is strangely arousing, and I swallow as coils of pleasure begin tightening in my belly. I widen my legs a little further, and a trickle of sweat runs down between my breasts. The tongue is insistent, flicking hard on my clit, and won't let up.

The tingling pleasure grows and builds to breaking point.

'Oh sweet Jesus, I'm going to come,' I groan.

Yet as soon as I say that, the tongue is removed in a flash. I moan petulantly and waggle my arse, wanting it back.

'No, Sadie, you will not climax,' Darius says throatily behind me.

'But ... I must ... please.' My thighs quiver in need. It's been so long since someone's concentrated on me and not thought about their own selfish pleasure.

'No, Sadie, you will not,' he repeats. 'Or there will be a severe punishment.'

I blink. 'Punishment?'

'Yes, a severe *painful* punishment. You will not like it. Promise me that you won't climax.'

I lick my lips. Thinking about this. How bad could this punishment be? Surely, it's worth the risk, and I *really* want this orgasm. He's got me so worked up that I know it's going to be knee-bucklingly good. What's it to him if I do anyway?

'All right, I promise I won't climax,' I lie. 'It will be difficult, mind you, because of your talented tongue. But I won't.'

He huffs a laugh. 'Good girl. If you can hold out for the next five minutes, until the clock chimes midnight, there will be an even greater pleasure for you than my tongue.'

I perk up at those words. Oooh, it's a test. And no doubt 'greater pleasure' means his cock. And I want that now Darius has proven his sexual prowess. He's going to be a great fuck.

But how the hell am I going to not come in the next five minutes? I'm right on the edge! It's impossible. I'm going to need something painful to distract me. Something sharp or—

'Ready?' intones Darius, his voice laced with humour and challenge.

'Yes,' I say, determined to win his approval and get my reward. 'I'm ready.'

His cold tongue plunges into my cunny. I clench my jaw, willing him to stay the hell away from my clit, and ...

He doesn't. He laps and circles it, and I can't help moaning at how good it feels. Heat pools in my lower belly, and tingles run up and down my spine. But I refuse to let him beat me. I grit my teeth and will my hips not to buck against the aching intensity.

The clock's hour hand inches forward. It's almost at twelve. If I can just hold out ... a bit longer ... his cock will be mine. Cold lips have replaced his tongue, and he sucks gently on my clit while his tongue wriggles inside my cunny, lapping at a certain sensitive spot over and over. Ohhh. Noooo. *Quickly, Sadie, think of shit, vomit, piss—of dirty feet, of the stink of Covent Garden's streets on a hot summer's day!*

I'm managing to stay afloat with this imagery when Darius increases the tempo of his tongue and sucks hard on my clit. It's too much. I can feel myself starting to fall apart.

'Fuck. You,' I pant, sweat pouring off my body from desire, the effort of trying not to come, and the heat radiating from the rising flames. Darius's mocking laugh from the depths of my cunny snaps something primal in me. I will not let this man break me. And I won't call out his name. Not now. Not ever. Steeling my nerves, I edge my hand towards the roaring fire.

Chapter 12

Sadie | Edinburgh, 1983

Pausing in front of Tim's door, I gather my thoughts before knocking. He's invited me upstairs this evening for some 'quality time', so I assume he wants a fuck. No, that's unfair of me. Tim's a nice guy. It's not his fault that he's involved with a vampire bitch with a hidden agenda, namely feeding on him when he's asleep. But if it wasn't him, it would be someone else. Hopefully, Elliott's about to change all that for us. I'm finding it difficult not to sink my fangs into him for a quick fix—I just know he's going to taste yummy. But I'm being a good little bloodsucker and letting him adjust to his new situation. It's a 'settle in first, bite later' scenario.

This invite to Tim's has come at an opportune time. Elliott needs new clothes, and Tim has a wardrobe full of stuff he doesn't wear, and they're about the same size. I've got my story down pat ...

'I've been busy. My cousin is in town and staying with us,' I say in reply to Tim's query about what I've been up to. We're in the kitchen, and I'm sitting at the table with my legs crossed, sipping delicately from a glass of white wine he's poured for me. It tastes like battery acid, but I drink it anyway to keep up the pretence that I'm a normal human being.

Tim bustles around, tossing various pinches of herbs into a simmering pan and tasting from a wooden spoon.

He must've come straight from the office as he's still in his business shirt with the sleeves rolled up and pinstripe trousers, an apron hastily tied over the top of the ensemble. Is he a stockbroker? An accountant? It's something that requires a pinstripe suit anyway.

'Ah, so that's why you haven't been replying to my calls,' he replies, stirring vigorously and sounding miffed. Tim's the only one who insists on ringing our flat. Occasionally, I'll pick up if I'm walking past because I can sense it's him. But most often, I don't if I can't tell who's calling—just in case it's the police, a blackmailer, or, worse, Alexander Dryden, Floss's grudge-bearing sire. So far, we've managed to avoid a run-in with *him*. But one of these days, we're going to have to face off—I can feel it in my stone-cold bones.

I shrug. 'Elliott hasn't been to Edinburgh before, so

we've been doing quite a bit of sightseeing.'

Tim throws me an enquiring look. 'Elliott. So it's a guy cousin?'

I nod. 'Yeah, and I know this is going to sound a bit odd. But do you have any spare clothes he can borrow? He kind of turned up unprepared for ... the weather. We could go shopping, but that's going to interfere with our sightseeing, and he's only here for two weeks.'

'Sure, we can have a look in my room before dinner. The coq au vin needs to simmer.' Tim turns down the heat on the stove.

I look at the pan on the stove, and my lips thin. Oh, so he's cooking for two. I really hate it when he assumes I'm staying for dinner as then I have to eat human food. Some of it tastes OK, like red meat, but chicken is foul (no pun intended). I told him I'm on the monotrophic diet, which involves eating only one food item. But he doesn't listen to me and says I need to eat properly, or I'll get sick.

But if I have to eat his coq au vin, so be it. Elliott needs to get kitted out.

'What's his style?' Tim enquires, leading the way to his bedroom.

'Uh, dunno. Casual, I guess?' I reply as he slides open the pine-panelled wardrobe door that stretches along the left-hand wall. Inside are hangers of neatly pressed shirts and suits, designer for business and linen for casual, and shelves of jeans and T-shirts. While he's rifling through his clothes, I sit on the super king-sized bed. The bedding smells of him— Old Spice aftershave and Imperial Leather soap. I've been in here plenty of times, and it never fails to amaze me how neat and tidy he is; there's not a pair of dirty socks on the floor or a bodybuilding magazine out of place on the nightstand. His *Playboy*s are safely out of sight in the cupboard, but I know they're there because I read his mind, and he feels guilty that he looks at them. He thinks I'd be upset if I knew.

Honestly? I don't give a shit if he wants to look at 2D tits and pussy.

I lean back on the bed, propping myself up on my elbows as Tim pulls out various items, muttering to himself. I'd love a top-floor bedroom like this. It's spacious and airy with cream carpet and cornflower-blue walls. A big white-framed bay window with a tartan padded seat looks out onto a leafy park. It's south facing, but too much sun isn't really an issue in Edinburgh, even in summer. Sitting on the window seat on a grey day, watching the rain clouds roll in across the treetops would be soothing. I think about my poky basement room and feel a twinge of jealousy. Oh well, one day.

At least I have a hot guy currently inhabiting my room,

even if he doesn't want to be there. I should probably feel guilty about that ...

Tim flops a load of clothes on the bed next to me and says, 'Will any of this do? They're clean. I just don't wear them anymore.'

I look through them briefly. Apart from jeans and T-shirts, he's included some smart jumpers and a dark-blue coat as well. 'Yeah, thanks. Elliott will be grateful to have some warm stuff to wear.' *Otherwise, he'll have to make do with a hot water bottle with a pink knitted cover.*

'What did he actually bring with him?' asks Tim curiously.

'Er, a T-shirt and a pair of jeans, and he's wearing those.'

Tim scrunches up his handsome face. 'He knew he was coming to Edinburgh for two weeks in winter, and he didn't pack any clothes?'

'He's staunch,' I reply. 'He's from Orkney.'

'Oh.' Tim doesn't look convinced. It does sound a bit suspect, I have to admit. He glances at me lying on the bed, and a flicker of desire crosses his face. His thoughts are torn between making out and concern that his coq au vin will burn. I play on that as I don't particularly want to get intimate at the moment.

I lift my nose into the air and sniff. 'Can you smell something?'

'Shit,' Tim mutters and races off to the kitchen. I gather up the clothes in my arms and trail after him, calculating how long I need to stay for the sake of politeness. I really need to get back to Elliott and see to his dinner. I've been feeding him peanut butter sandwiches, but he's getting angry about that. Ooh, maybe I can say I'm not feeling well and get some of the coq au vin to go?

I lean against the doorjamb while Tim stirs and tastes from the pot again. 'Any chance I could get dinner to go? It smells great.'

He turns and stares at me. 'What?'

'I'm not feeling too well, time of the month and all that. But I might be able to manage some of it later on. Sorry, I know you've gone to a lot of trouble.'

Tim's mouth tightens. He yanks open a nearby drawer, rummages around noisily, and grabs a Tupperware container. With a pair of tongs, he takes out two chicken legs, chucks them into the container, and slops in a few spoonfuls of the gravy, then adds some vegetables and rice. He bangs on the lid of the container and holds it out to me. 'Here,' he snaps.

I take the container and place it on top of my armful of clothes. 'Thanks.' I feel a bit bad, but I didn't ask him to cook for me. There's no need to have a temper tantrum.

Tim's jaw is clenched, and his brow is corrugated.

'Well, I guess I should—' I say, taking a step backwards.

'Do you even like me, Sadie?' he blurts.

I hitch a shoulder defensively. 'Of course I like you. Why even ask that?'

He folds his arms and glares at me. 'Because from where I'm standing, I'm not getting that impression. You want to see me when it's convenient for you. I think you're using me.'

I readjust the clothes, trying to keep the container from sliding off. What he said is true actually. I can't deny it. For the last six months, I've been coming up here for sex and a feed (and I don't mean his home cooking).

But I don't do well with confrontation. He's backing me into a corner.

'Perhaps it's best we break up then,' I say calmly. 'If you feel like that.'

Tim's lips part, and his eyes widen. 'I didn't mean—'

'Yeah,' I say, getting on a roll. 'This isn't really working for me. And being forced into having dinner when I'm feeling ill with period cramps, well ... that's not cool.'

Tim runs a hand through his hair, looking distressed. 'I'm sorry, I didn't mean to be insensitive. I don't want to break up.'

I humph and look away.

He says more softly, 'You mean a lot to me, Sadie.'

'We've been seeing each other casually. It's hardly a committed relationship,' I say weakly.

But it is nice to have a convenient blood source upstairs. And he's not bad in bed either.

Tim takes off his apron and hangs it on the back of a kitchen chair. The frown is gone and has been replaced by a look of mild apprehension. 'What I'm about to say will hopefully change that. I was going to do this during dinner, but since you're taking dinner with you ...' He dives into his suit trouser pocket and drops down onto one knee.

Oooh, wow. Shit!

'Sadie Bouffant, I love you. Will you marry me?' Tim beseeches.

I gaze at the red velvet box he's presenting. It contains a diamond ring and not a cheap one either by the looks of it. He makes good money doing whatever he does in his suits, so he can afford it.

I swallow and kick myself for not breaking up with him sooner. Even if I did have feelings for him, there's no way I can marry him. He doesn't even know I'm a vampire.

'That's a lovely gesture, Tim. But I'm sorry, my answer is no,' I state.

'Just like that? You won't even think about it?' His frown is back.

'You're a great guy, Tim, and I like you a lot. But I won't make you happy...'

'You *do* make me happy!' he says emphatically.

'I'm a free spirit. I hate being tied down ...'

'You're just afraid—'

I can't help laughing at that. Me, afraid! I'm not afraid. He has no idea who I am. I can slam a grown man against the wall.

Tim leaps to his feet and shoves the ring back in his pocket. 'You think this is a joke?' he says angrily. 'That my feelings are a joke?'

'I don't,' I say hurriedly. 'It was just—'

'Get out,' he says. 'I don't know why I'm even bothering. You have no feelings for me. You're a stone-cold freak.'

Pain stabs my unbeating heart. Ouch, OK, that hurt. I growl softly in the back of my throat. I've a good mind to show this human some manners. But I rein myself in. Tim is a nice person in general, and he's only lashing out because he's upset. He doesn't deserve to be ripped to shreds for that.

'You need to go out with someone else and forget about me,' I force myself to say gently. 'I'm only going to end up hurting you.'

Tim looks at me and doesn't reply.

'Thanks for the clothes. I'll make sure that—'

'Your cousin can keep them,' Tim interrupts gruffly.

'Well, OK. Thanks.' I take a step backwards. 'Goodbye,

Tim. I'm sorry.'

He stares at me morosely while the the coq au vin bubbles away on the stove. From the smell of it, I do think it's actually burning now. But I don't comment, just leave.

As I walk towards the front door, I spot a red Walkman lying on the sideboard and put that on top of the Tupperware container. Tim can easily buy another one, and I'm sure Elliott will appreciate having some music to listen to.

After managing to get out of Tim's flat with all his stuff, I lean against the wall and close my eyes. Fuck, that was awkward. Why did Tim have to go and propose right then and there? It's completely my fault. I shouldn't have let it go as far as it did. I knew he was thinking along those lines. But I wanted to keep enjoying myself, and it was nice to have him pursuing me. Now I'm not going to see him again. Ever. Unless I bump into him in the stairwell or the entranceway or outside ... Hmm, I think I need to call a flat meeting. We're going to have to move.

CHAPTER 13

Sadie | Highlands, present day

'The fuel light has come on,' says Damian, nodding to the dashboard as we reach the outskirts of Perth. 'Everyone OK if I pull into the first petrol station we come to?'

'Yes, of course,' answers Floss for the rest of us. The atmosphere in the car up until this point has been tense, to say the least. I've given up on trying to get Damian to drive faster, though I did compel him at one point to press down harder on the accelerator to at least get up to seventy miles an hour. But he freaked out, and Floss yelled at me to stop it. I've been sulking in silence ever since.

'Are we even going the right way?' Hester asks. 'Should we do another hypnosis session to find out?'

'Probably a good idea,' says Damian, his hazel eyes flicking to mine in the rear-view mirror. 'But we should wait until we're in a more private location. Practising hypnosis on someone in a petrol station is bound to attract attention.'

I give a sharp nod. 'Fine.'

The buzzing is still strong in my mind, which is something. If only I could pick up on words or images from Elliott, then I wouldn't have to undergo this stupid hypnosis. Yet not being able to read his thoughts is why I never got bored with him—I could do what I liked with his body, which was always mine to control. He'd work tirelessly for me and willingly submit to my bite, even hungered for it, but I could never break his mind. He was an endless source of intrigue to me in that respect. Then again, I shouldn't be thinking of him in the past tense. He is still very much alive. For the meantime.

The sky is the colour of gunmetal as Damian indicates and pulls into a Shell station. 'I'm going to grab a snack after filling up,' he says when we're parked in one of the pump bays. 'Anyone want anything?'

Three pairs of eyes stare intently at his neck, and he swallows. 'Uh, right. Perhaps a blood bag to share from the boot?' His gaze slides to Floss. 'Or a little feed from me ...?'

'We're fine for now. Just sort yourself out,' Floss replies, her jaw visibly tightening from the effort of holding back her fangs. I can sense her arousal too. The merest suggestion of biting him and her bloodlust is raring to go.

I smirk to myself and remark to Hester, *If Damian isn't a*

vampire by the end of this trip, I'll be mightily surprised. His blood really gets her horny.

Hester: *Well, when it's true love.*

Me (scoffing): *True love? True lust more like! They hardly know each other.*

Hester: *Does time make a difference? You should know better than anyone about fated mates ...*

Me: *What are you saying?*

Hester: *That you and Elliott—*

Me (sharply): *That is purely a business arrangement. This conversation is over.*

Aloud, I say, 'I'm going for a short walk to clear my head.'

'OK, but don't go too far,' says Floss, who's been completely oblivious to my telepathic conversation with Hester. Or I think she has. But if she's started reading Damian's mind, it's a sign her mental powers are getting stronger. I'm going to have to be more careful about talking about her behind her back.

Outside, the pungent smell of gasoline hits my nostrils; and along with my hunger, it makes me feel queasy. I wander over towards the bushes lining the tarmac to get away from the stench and let the fresh cold breeze wash over me. Having filled up, Damian is inside paying at the counter for the petrol and his snacks.

There's a rustle behind me, and I twist around, peering

into the bushes. If it's a squirrel, maybe I can get a quick fix without the others seeing. My fangs ache at the thought of warm fresh blood. But scrabbling around in the bushes in a skirt and high heels isn't exactly ladylike. And my tights will get snagged. (Yes, I'm dressed suitably for the occasion. Just because it's a road trip, I'm not going to wear hiking gear—*quelle horreur!*)

Then a cheery whistle floats to my ears, and I snap my head around to see something much better than a flea-infested squirrel in my line of sight. A bearded dude, tall and broad-chested, has emerged from the driver's seat of a Graham's milk truck and is striding towards the restrooms.

Oooh, what do we have here? I sniff and catch the scent of his blood. It smells rich and full of protein, like he's been gorging on Greggs sausage rolls for breakfast.

A beagle on the hunt, I trail him across the cracked concrete, mouth watering. This is a bad idea on so many levels. But bloodlust is flooding my system, and it's the higher calling that I always obey. Plus I need to keep my strength up. Damian can scoff his Pringles. This is my midmorning snack.

The guy is midstream in a urinal when I barge through the door. He glances round and drawls in a thick Scottish accent, 'Lasses are next door.' He carries on pissing, unconcerned.

When I don't move or reply, he glances round again with a quirked eyebrow; his gaze takes in my crop top, short skirt, and high heels.

Finishing his business, he shakes his cock but doesn't poke it back into his jeans. Deliberately, he turns to face me with his dick hanging out, and my eyes drop to it. It's long and girthy with several prominent purple veins. Nestled in black wiry hair, it's semi-erect, which suggests that a pretty blonde looking at his dick is turning him on. 'Sticking around coz you like what you see, gorgeous?' he says, voice thickening.

Yup, that confirms it. Typical. He wants his dick sucked. But I'm more interested in a thorough suck from his neck, so he's shit out of luck.

I run my tongue over my lips, staring intently at his member, causing it to harden further. Then I smile pleasantly and nod in agreement.

Grinning, he takes a step towards me, cock bobbing; and I shove him back against the flimsy wall with my mind before he can get any closer. His eyes widen in fear when he discovers he can't move a muscle. I take my time sauntering over to him.

'Your cock's OK ...' I say, grasping it in one hand and leaning in closer to sniff his neck. I run my tongue along the line of his T-shirt, tasting the salt of his sweat. Adrenaline is now coursing through his veins, and his thoughts are a mix of regret that he decided to show me his cock and wanting to strangle me with his bare fists. Gosh, what a caveman; must be all that hairy testosterone between his legs. I squeeze his dick hard in my fist, and a gurgle emits from his lips. '… But it's definitely not the prettiest I've seen.'

Elliott's cock is gorgeous. Smiling dreamily at a recent memory of being fucked senseless by my thrall and wanting all this Alexander hideousness to go away, I bare my fangs. Inching closer, I lean in and prick his smooth neck with the sharp tips. Lower down his throat, there's not as much hair. But his beard is pretty bushy. Dark black like his pubes. A few beads of blood form on his neck; and I lap at them blissfully, unable to help sinking my fangs in deeper, angling for his jugular. The trucker moans in fear, but his cock is hard in my hand and oozing pre-cum. Ooh, he likes that, does he? I might give him a handjob while I'm feeding—

'*Sadie!*' Damian's shocked voice rings out behind me.

Damn, he would choose now to take a piss.

'Fuck off!' I snarl, my lips and tongue coated in blood. 'I'm feeding.'

A large hand grips my shoulder like a vice, and Damian says in a stern tone, 'Back away from the trucker, Sadie.'

I shake my head and adjust my grip on the trucker's slippery cock, keeping a tight hold of my prey. 'No, he's mine. I found him first. You can't have him.'

Hunger is warping my mind because I can't satiate it. So I'm bloodlust babbling to Damian, like he's a'vampire, like he's going to take my quarry. It's a thing that happens sometimes if you're not careful to keep up with regular feeds, though I can't remember it happening to me like this for a while. My Elliott keeps me beautifully satisfied. Satisfied so I don't create situations ... like this.

Damian keeps talking to me in a low steady voice, some nonsense about letting the dude go (as if!). But he does so warily, as if he knows I could just as easily turn around and launch at him. Slowly, his words—skipping like white smooth common-sense stones across the fiery red pool of my mind—sink in fully; and I release my grip on the trucker's cock so it flops between his legs.

'That's good. Very good, Sadie. Now take a step backwards.'

Me (whimpering, my eyes fixed on the trucker's neck): *But. His. Lovely. Blood.*

Damian: *There's plenty of blood waiting for you in the car. You can even feed from me a little if you like.*

I perk up at that. Floss will really get her knickers in a twist if I feed from her boyfriend. It will be fun to rile her.

Me: *Pinky promise?*

Damian: *Pinky promise. Now let him go.*

With a grunt, I release the trucker from his position against the wall, and he falls to his knees with a gasp and bursts into tears of relief.

Damian grabs my hand and quickly hauls me out of the bathroom. 'You need to memory-wipe him asap!'

'Of course!' I scoff. 'Though you should have zipped up his jeans. He's going to wonder why he's on his knees, sobbing with his dick out.'

CHAPTER 14

Elliott | Highlands, present day

Everything aches. After a dreamless doze, I awake in gloom, sprawled on hard slabs. Groggily, my eyes lift to the small barred window high above my head letting in a smidgeon of light. From where I'm lying, I can see the outlines of rough-hewn walls. The space isn't large, but it's compact and empty apart from me. I'm in a dim stone chamber. A dungeon cell. The ground is strewn with straw, but the cold still seeps through my hips and butt. Shivering, I shift position and become aware of a heavy weight on my left arm. An iron shackle is clipped tightly around my wrist. Fuck, seriously? I mean, is that really necessary?

I yank at the short chain that's attached to the wall behind me and call out weakly for help. No one comes, and I lie back, feeling exhausted even from that short burst of activity. I'm determined not to give in to my fear, but it's difficult not to. What does Alexander want from me? It can't be simply that he's hungry, or he would have drained me. There must be another reason ...

Fuck, I'm going to die in this pit, and I'll never see Sadie again. Why the hell didn't she turn me? It's a question I've been asking myself for the last forty years.

I try to feel annoyed at her, but I can't. It's not her fault that Alexander's kidnapped me. I mean Sadie's done her best over the last century to help Floss and Hester evade this dickwad. But if I were a vampire, things might be different. I might have been able to fight him off or, if not that, at least communicate with her. I try yelling at her in my mind that I'm alive, but there's no reply. I don't expect one since we can't speak to each other telepathically. And what use is it anyway if I don't even know where I am?

The memory of Sadie's terrified face floats into my mind as I was dragged kicking and screaming from her bed. Thankfully, I was fully clothed in a T-shirt, jeans, and trainers. I shudder to think what would have happened if things had been further along when Alexander strolled in. It would've been a case of lying in the back seat of his car butt naked. I was barely conscious and weak after Alexander dragged me in there and continued sucking on my neck from the holes he'd opened in Sadie's bedroom. After that, he hopped in the driver's seat and took off. I must've passed out, but I came to briefly when he was driving along some motorway. Alexander had switched on the radio and was flipping around the stations. He settled on a U2 song and sang along loudly with Bono about still not finding what he was looking for—making me wince and wish I had earplugs. He truly is a crap singer. I hope he doesn't frequent any karaoke bars. He'd be booed off the stage.

The hinges of the iron-studded door in the corner of the room creak; and I tense, struggling upright, straining to see in the dim light.

'Hello? Is anyone there?'

Tentative footsteps ensue, and a young woman in her twenties shuffles into the room with a tray of food. I sigh in relief. Thank God, another person and something to eat at last! But as the woman inches closer, I get a shock. She's a walking corpse. Her long shoulder-length brown hair is lank and tangled and frames a thin pale face, large haunted eyes, and hollow cheeks. What's even more disturbing is that she's wearing a saucy French maid's outfit: a short ruffled black silk dress with a low-cut neckline. Not that she has any breasts to speak of—her body is skin and bones. Her bare feet scuff along the straw, and they're filthy.

The young woman bends, knees creaking, and deposits the tray wordlessly next to me. Close enough that I can reach it, but not so close that I can grab her. 'Thanks,' I say, but she doesn't reply. I look up at her, attempting to make some sort of eye contact. But her grey eyes are glazed over.

Great, she's completely in thrall to Alexander, which explains a lot. I spot two blood-encrusted wounds on her neck where he's been feeding. I feel like showing her mine. *Look, matchy-matchy.*

She shuffles back over to the door. I think that's it for her visit, but then she's back again, with a wooden bucket dangling from her fingers. This is placed next to the tray, I assume for my 'ablutions'. *Shitting in a bucket and having to lie next to it. Great, just how I like to spend my dungeon day.*

There's more shuffling, and she's heading out the door. The hinges creak.

'Wait!' I cry.

The girl halts. Slowly, she turns her thin form and waits as I've instructed. OK, if she's being dutiful to me, maybe I can find out some information.

'What does Alexander want with me?'

There's a pause. Then the girl hitches a shoulder and intones in a flat voice, 'I don't know.'

I try again.

'Are there more women like you here?'

She nods once.

'How many are there?'

'Many.'

'Like ten or twenty?'

She hitches a shoulder. 'Many.'

OK, I'm not getting too far with that line of questioning.

I hold up my iron-shackled wrist. 'Can you get a key to unlock this?'

'No, I only do my master's bidding,' she intones lifelessly.

I run my eyes over her skimpy French maid's outfit. I can imagine what he bids her to do in that. The fucker. I mean, I know I'm in thrall to Sadie, but at least she doesn't make me dress up like a male stripper. She's sensible with her demands.

The young woman (I'm starting to think of her as Agnes for some reason) lifts a bony finger and points at the wooden tray, which has a white bowl of brown lumpy soup and some hard-looking sourdough bread sitting alongside. No butter. 'He says eat ... Please.' I'm not sure if that last word is solely hers or Alexander's attempt at conveying some manners.

Agnes shuffles out the door, and it clangs shut and locks.

I sigh and drag the tray closer, dip in the bread, and take a bite. It's canned stew. Barely warm and not great. Sadie would be disgusted. I get a clear image of her rolling her eyes in mock disdain and saying, '*Quelle horreur*, Elliott. What izzz that sheet?'

I grin. We've certainly come a long way from those early days when she made me peanut butter sandwiches and I flung them against her bedroom wall. I can still see the look on Sadie's face as a sandwich stuck to the pink paint, then fell off, leaving a poo-like stain. It was very satisfying at the time. Of course, I wouldn't do anything like that now. But it's a funny memory, and I laugh to myself as I eat. It makes me feel better—like she's here with me.

CHAPTER 15

Elliott | Edinburgh, 1983

Sadie waltzes into the bedroom, her arms laden with clothes. She dumps a bundle of T-shirts and jeans on the end of the bed. There are jumpers and a coat too.

'Don't say I don't do anything for you. Check out this haul,' she says, looking pleased with herself.

Dutifully, I peer at the pile of items. I'm sitting cross-legged, propped against the headboard, reading a *Smash Hits* magazine I found on Sadie's bedside table. There's an article about Duran Duran, which initially gave me heart palpitations. The Sing Blue Silver Tour continued without me! Everyone obviously bought the story about the genital herpes. But somehow, I can't summon any effort to care. That's my old life, and this is now my reality.

'What's all this for?'

'You! It's your new wardrobe. You can't keep wearing the same T-shirt and jeans. And besides'—Sadie wrinkles her nose—'they're starting to smell.'

I reach over and pick up a light-blue T-shirt and finger the alligator logo. It looks expensive and brand new. 'Did you go shopping for me?'

I find that hard to believe. I haven't seen or heard any of the women who live in this flat go outside. Unless they do when I'm asleep. Anything's possible. They seem to like staying up late. Sadie herself keeps very strange hours. I've never seen her sleep. She seems to have given up her bed to me.

I've been keeping my eyes and ears open ever since the conversation in the lounge about how they needed blood. That freaked the hell out of me, and they saw that it had and didn't say anything more. So I still don't know what they're planning to do with me. I'm starting to think all of them have escaped from a mental hospital. The police and the prison psychiatrists will be very interested, I'm sure. So I'm taking a lot of mental notes when I'm not sleeping or complaining. The other day, I asked for a notepad and pen, saying I wanted to jot down some song ideas. But Sadie gave me a funny look, and after that, I forgot that I'd asked for it in the first place.

'No, they're from the guy upstairs. He said he didn't want them.' Something about the way Sadie says this makes me perk up my ears. There's a guardedness to her tone.

'A friend?' I ask casually.

She shrugs and averts her eyes, but not before I catch a flash of pain. Oh, he's hurt her somehow. The thought of it instantly brings out my protective side, though I don't know why. She's nothing to me.

'Did something happen with him? Is he your boyfriend?'

Sadie flops into the small armchair by the window and looks glum. 'Not anymore. I *was* seeing him,' she admits. 'But it got ... messy. We had a fight.' She chews her bottom lip distractedly.

'Not because of me?' I ask. If this guy knows I exist, then maybe I have a chance of being rescued.

She shakes her head. 'No, it was about something else.'

Oh, damn. No luck there then.

'Maybe you'll patch things up,' I say hopefully.

'I don't think so. It's definitely over. But look in the left coat pocket.'

Hesitantly, I put my hand into the pocket, expecting a mousetrap to go off or something. It's the kind of sick joke she'd play. But my fingers touch plastic, something spongy, and cool metal. Slowly, I draw out the object and discover it's a red Walkman with orange earphones.

'I thought you might like to listen to some music. There should be a tape in there, but I don't know what it is.'

I flip open the cassette holder and chuckle when I see what the tape is.

Sadie cocks an eyebrow. 'What's so funny?'

'It's *Rio*, by Duran Duran.'

She giggles. 'No way! I didn't know Tim liked them. The sly devil. He was always going on about Roxy Music and Simple Minds and said that Duran Duran was poncy.'

I frown at that. 'Poncy! They're not poncy.'

'Yeah, I don't feel too bad stealing his Walkman now!'

'*What*? You stole his Walkman?'

She shrugs. 'It seemed like recompense for what he said to me.' Again, the pained look.

I don't press her for details on that. It was obviously something mean. This Tim guy sounds like a right knob.

'Well, if that's his attitude, you're better off without him.' I press play on the Walkman, put on the earphones and the catchy intro to 'Hungry Like the Wolf' starts playing softly. 'Oh, I love this song,' I say and can't help smiling. I tap my foot, itching for her to go now so I can lose myself in the music.

'Me too,' agrees Sadie with a nod. '"Hungry Like the Wolf" is the best song on the album.' Wow, she must have good hearing to detect it from all the way over there!

'I'll leave you to listen in peace.' She pushes up off the chair and strolls to the door. When she reaches it, she throws me a glance. 'Oh, I forgot to say. You're getting coq au vin for dinner.'

My stomach rumbles hearing that. If I have to eat another peanut butter sandwich, I'm going to vomit all over the bedclothes in protest. New clothes, Duran Duran, *and* coq au vin. This is turning out to be a great day!

CHAPTER 16

Sadie | London, 1758

I howl and jerk my hand away from the flames as the tips of my fingers sear. Before I know what's happening, Darius has whipped me over to the bed and is gently laying me down. 'Ow, it hurts!' I moan, thrashing my naked limbs about.

'Lie still,' Darius grunts, inspecting the damage. He prods at my blistered pink fingers, and I gasp in pain, gathering my hand to my chest.

'You silly girl, Sadie. Why did you go and do that?'

'Because ... because,' I moan.

'Confess. It was because you didn't want to climax and have me win and inflict my punishment upon you.'

I stop thrashing and lift my gaze to his. Hmm, he seems to have got the measure of me quite easily. 'Peerrrhappps ...' My gaze drops to his breeches, where his erection is quite obvious. I lick my lips, burnt fingers half forgotten. I can smear some butter on them later. 'So do I win the prize?'

Darius nods slowly. 'Of course.' He gazes at my blistered flesh. 'Since you went to such lengths to obtain it. I retract my insult. What a clever girl you are.'

I preen in triumph at his words, my cunny twinging in anticipation. Oooh goody, it's cock o'clock. This is going to be worth the agony.

'Let me undress first, though,' he says throatily. 'You may watch if you so desire.'

I nod eagerly. *Oh, I do desire.*

Darius rises and, facing me, unbuttons his blood-red waistcoat. He shrugs it off, places it on a coat hanger, and pops it in the wardrobe. Then his shirt is unbuttoned ... excruciatingly slowly ... button by button flipped from their tiny holes.

Come on, I think, wriggling in impatience. *Get to the good bit.*

He smirks as if he knows what I'm thinking.

The shirt is off (finally!), and I gasp in appreciation. The man's body is perfection: smooth milky skin, strong wide shoulders, and a narrow waist. His chest has a smattering of dark hair and his abdomen is ridged with muscle. The black snake tattoo that I saw inked on his forearm winds its way up his right arm and disappears over his shoulder—the head of it nowhere in sight.

He undoes a single button on his breeches (ever so

slowly). They hang there on his hips, suspended by his monstrous bulge, while Darius folds his shirt, doing up each button, ensuring it's neat and tidy. This is placed carefully on a shelf in a nearby cupboard. I nearly groan in frustration. *For God's sake, man, you're not a maid!*

Darius huffs a laugh.

Sweet Jesus, he's enjoying teasing me and making me want him. My breath shallows at this knowledge, and despite my annoyance, moisture gathers in my cunny. It remembers having his tongue lapping down there and wants his cock. *Now.* I squirm, rubbing my thighs together, and let out an exasperated sigh.

'Did you say something, Sadie?'

'Darius, please,' I beg. 'I don't like waiting. Remove your breeches.'

He grins. 'Now why would I do that?' he taunts.

'Um ...' I lift an eyebrow and tilt my head at his twitching crotch. 'Isn't your cock my prize? I really want my prize ... right here,' I purr, parting my thighs and rubbing along my creamy cunny with two fingers so he can see what's in store for him. Lots of my regulars like it when I do this. It drives them wild, and for some, it speeds up the sex act by at least ten minutes. But Darius doesn't move a muscle, though he is staring intently at my wet cunny.

'No,' he says after a pause. 'My cock isn't your prize, so

you can close your legs.'

'Oh.' I snap my thighs shut like a clam. 'So why are you getting undressed then?'

'So blood doesn't stain my shirt. It's hard to get out.'

I stare at him. 'W-what?'

He grins at me. 'Oh, Sadie, you're in for such a treat. I almost wish I was you ...'

From this, I'm really not sure what is going to happen. And I've suddenly noticed his teeth. A couple of them are big, white, and shiny—like he's having trouble keeping his lips closed. Were they like that before? Surely, I would have noticed. Then again, he's had his face planted in my nether regions for most of the evening. We haven't exactly chatted. But if we're not going to fuck, what's the point of being here? What a waste of time.

'Oh well,' I say, swinging my legs off the bed. 'The night is young. I'm sure I can find someone else to—'

Before my toes touch the floor, my ankles are gripped by an unseen force and swivelled back onto the bed. It feels like something is clamping around them, but there's nothing there. My hands lift out to either side of the bed and are pinned to the bedcovers. But by what, I have no idea. I'm now spreadeagled on my back, unable to move.

'What are you ... Let me go!' I jerk and twist against the invisible restraints, but it's in vain. I'm held fast.

'Lie still,' Darius commands.

I cry out as pincer-like claws squeeze my brain, then ease off. For the first time this evening, I feel truly afraid.

'Who the hell are you?' I gasp.

Darius smiles as he walks towards the bed. 'A customer you'll never forget.'

Chapter 17

Sadie | Highlands, present day

Drops of rain splatter the tarmac as Damian opens the car door and shoves me into the back seat.

He starts the engine, and we take off with a squeal of rubber. Floss throws him a querying look from the passenger seat. 'What's the hurry, babe?'

She and Hester were facing away from the men's loo, so they didn't see Damian yanking me away from it—and the unfortunate trucker. The taste of his blood is on my tongue, so it'll be easy enough to wipe his memory before we get too far out of range. He'll be back in his Graham's milk truck shortly, none the wiser about what happened when he went off to take an innocent piss. But he may wonder why his neck hurts.

'Apart from Elliott being in mortal danger, I checked the weather, and it's not looking great. I don't want to hang around,' Damian replies calmly without even a wobble in his voice to betray any of what just happened. I'm impressed. I feel a bit better now that the bloodlust has subsided, and I apologise (albeit grudgingly).

Me: *Thanks for pulling me away from that guy and for not telling the others what I did. They don't need to know about it. It'll be our little secret. Quick thinking about the weather too.*

Damian: *I did actually check the weather, and I don't want to keep secrets from Floss. I'll probably tell her later on.*

Me: *Oh, right. But you'll still let me feed from you? You did promise.*

Damian: *Fine. You get five minutes. That's all.*

His jaw clenches, and his knuckles turn white on the steering wheel. I back out of his mind space hastily, sensing his annoyance about having agreed to that. Well, too bad! If he's going to be one of us, he'll need to learn that you can't break promises once you make them. It's a coven rule.

Now that he's agreed to it, I can't help staring at Damian's neck and its visibly pulsing vein. His adrenaline is heightened, and he's going through a moral dilemma about letting me feed from him and how to tell Floss about it. I don't care about any of that. My mouth is watering. Floss is always in raptures over how good Damian's blood tastes, so I'm looking forward to sampling it for myself.

A thin drizzle begins as we leave Perth, and Damian heads north towards the Highlands without giving any reason for doing so. But no one disputes his decision. There's only one main road, so it makes sense that Alexander came this way.

After twenty minutes, the light is fading fast, though it's barely noon. Damian switches on his car lights and the windscreen wipers; one of them goes swish-squeak swish-squeak, and it sets my teeth on edge. Leaning forward, I peer through the windscreen to see ominous dark clouds ahead. The sky looks like it's about to explode—I can relate.

'We're driving into a storm,' I say pointlessly.

'No shit,' says Damian through gritted teeth. His neck muscles are now strained as he peers at the slick road; his speed has dropped right down again.

'What do you think, babe?' asks Floss, placing a hand on his leg.

Damian sighs. 'It might be better to wait it out and decide what to do next.'

His eyes flick to mine in the rear-view mirror briefly, then back to the road. 'My Uncle Tim's place is in Pitlochry, which isn't far from here. We can hole up there for the night so I can do a hypnosis session and see if Sadie can pick up anything more from Elliott.'

'No,' I say instantly. 'Not Tim. I don't want to go there.'

'It makes sense, Sadie,' says Hester. 'Do you want to find Elliott or not?'

'You know I do. It's just ... well ...' I feel sick at the thought of seeing Tim again after all these years. 'He kind of hates me,' I mutter. 'And how am I going to explain why I look exactly the same as when he last saw me in 1983?'

There's silence as everyone digests this. Hah! Not so keen on going there now, are we?

'Let's take a vote on it,' says Floss. 'Uncle Tim or a hotel. I vote for Uncle Tim.'

Damian nods. 'Me too. Uncle Tim.'

'My vote is for a hotel,' I state firmly. 'Preferably four-star or up. There are plenty of choices around here.' I'm quietly confident that will sway Hester as she's a sucker for a nice hotel with excellent amenities. I know this because we took a few trips to the Highlands before we bought our flat in Ramsay Garden to see if it was viable for us to stay up here and feed from animals. It was. But Floss refused point-blank to leave Edinburgh, so that plan fell through. We had several lovely stays in five-star hotels, though.

'My vote is for Uncle Tim,' says Hester, studiously avoiding my eyes.

Motherfucker!

CHAPTER 18

When we reach Pitlochry, Damian relays Tim's address, and Floss reads out directions from Google Maps on her phone. We turn left, right, left, left until we're driving down a narrow road that's practically a dirt track.

Through the rain-smeared window are low stone walls and damp green fields scattered with sheep. I screw up my nose. This really is the middle of nowhere. Why is Tim living out here? It doesn't escape my notice that if I'd turned him and married him, this could have been our off-grid vampire hidey-hole. There's something appealing about that. But there was Elliott to think of, and it would have meant abandoning Floss and—

Hester lets out a loud squeal, and we all jump in our seats. Damian jerks the wheel, and the car skids on the muddy track. I quickly scan the rear window, thinking that she's seen Alexander leaping over sheep or something. But she's staring fixedly at her phone.

'Jesus,' says Damian, shaking his head. 'Give me a warning if you're going to do that!'

'Sorry, I got excited,' Hester mumbles.

'What the fuck is it?' I growl.

'Yes, we're all ears,' says Floss.

'It's Will—he's a guy in my acting class,' Hester adds for Damian's benefit. 'He just sent us a group message. He's got the part of Orsino in *Twelfth Night* at the Globe in London! For a three-month stint!'

Oh, is that all? I think. *Hardly worth screaming about.* Out loud, I say, 'Good for him.'

Hester nods emphatically. 'Yes, it's like his dream role. But that's not all. He said the role of Viola is up for grabs too. The actress they had in mind has signed up for a Broadway production. They're holding auditions next week. And get this—they want a *tall* woman with *an English accent.*'

'Ooooh,' says Floss, turning around in her seat. 'You'd be perfect!'

'I know! And Viola ends up with Orsino. Well ... eventually, she does. Oh my god, I have to get that part! It means spending three months in London with Will!'

'Hester kind of likes Will,' Floss murmurs to Damian. 'If you hadn't picked up on that.'

'Ah,' he says with a nod, keeping his eyes on the road.

'But you get stage fright, and you can't even read aloud in class,' I state in a bemused voice. 'How are you going to perform in front of a packed theatre?'

Hester shrugs. 'I'll have to deal with it.'

'Have you ever actually acted in a play?' I ask. I think she told me once, but I've forgotten.

'Yes, of course, a few times. Most recently during the eighteenth century in Drury Lane.'

'How did that go?' asks Damian curiously.

Hester's green eyes flash, and her expression is stony. 'I had fruit pelted at me and was booed off the stage. It's taken a while to get over that experience. But this is the perfect chance to help me get back on track. And Will is *such* a good actor. He can bolster any supporting role ... And he's going to look great in a doublet and hose ...' She breaks off, looking dreamy.

'I'll help you with your lines when we get to Tim's while Damian is hypnotising Sadie,' says Floss encouragingly.

'Great, thanks. I'll get Will to send me a script!' She starts typing busily on her phone.

I rub my temple, which is starting to buzz and throb as if Elliott senses we're getting distracted.

'Hello?' I say sharply. 'You do know that rescuing Elliott is our top priority here!'

'Of course,' replies Hester. 'But there's going to be downtime tonight when Tim and Damian are asleep. We'll rescue Elliott and deal with Alexander. Then I can head to London for the audition. Easy-peasy!'

I close my eyes briefly and grit my teeth. She makes it sound like a done deal. I know I need to think positively, but I'm not that confident Elliott will still be alive by the time we get to him. And I'm not sure how I'm going to cope if he's not. I might have to face facts—that I'm not going to see him again.

Swallowing hard, I stare out the window and force myself to remember the good times. There are so many to choose from. Like when he finally cottoned on to the fact I was a vampire. I smirk to myself. That was hilarious. It was forty years ago, but I can still remember it as if it were yesterday ...

Chapter 19

Elliott | Edinburgh, 1983

'Are you drugging me?'

I'm lying on Sadie's bed, wearing one of the new/old T-shirts she brought me and a pair of the stonewashed jeans. The Duran Duran T-shirt I was wearing has been laundered and folded neatly, though. She seems to appreciate that it's my favourite.

Sadie is at the dressing table, brushing her hair. She lowers her brush, and her shocked blue eyes pierce mine. '*What?*'

I repeat my question. 'Are you drugging me?'

It's the logical conclusion I've come to after weeks of trying to figure out why I can't bring myself to leave the flat—she's turned me into a drug addict. I don't seem to care about anything else but living here with these three women and helping them in some way. But why I want to, and what exactly it is, is still beyond my grasp.

'If you are, it's OK,' I say when she doesn't reply. 'I

mean, it's not *OK* that I'm now an addict, but I understand. I just want to know what the drug is, or if it's more than one. Like, is it a combination of uppers and downers ...?'

Sadie's expression gives nothing away. She comes and sits next to me on the bed, and I shuffle my legs over to make room for her. Sometimes she lies next to me at night, but she's gone when I wake up in the morning. I've noted that she's a very quiet breather. Which is good as I'm a light sleeper. Well, I was. Now the drug makes me so relaxed that I pass out straightaway, even though I've been lying around doing nothing all day except listening to music or reading *Smash Hits.*

'Is it cocaine and Valium?' I press. That's all the drugs I know. Apart from weed. I saw various pills and 'special' cigarettes floating around when I was on the concert tour. I partook once or twice, but I'm a generally a clean-living guy. Besides, I had a responsibility to the band to remain clear-headed. A roadie operating on a drug-induced high would have been no use to anyone.

'I'm not giving you drugs, Elliott,' Sadie says, placing her pale white hands in her lap. She has nice nails. They're like little translucent shells and always buffed to a high shine.

'Then why can't I leave?' I whisper, feeling suddenly emotional about my situation. My throat bobs as I swallow a lump in my throat, and Sadie stares fixedly at my neck.

She's been doing that a lot lately.

'Do you want to know the truth?' she asks.

I nod and sigh with relief. 'Yes please. Just tell me. It's driving me crazy.'

'I'm sure it is.' She plucks at a thread on the bedcover, and I wait. I'm good at that. Patience is my forte, but even I have my limits. 'So the thing is', she says slowly, 'I can override your will and make you do things, Elliott. You're my thrall.'

I blink. 'T-thrall?'

'Yeah. Sorry, but our coven has certain ... needs that we need help with.'

'You mean the blood?'

She nods.

I rub my face, confused. The words 'thrall' and 'coven' and the need for 'blood' suggest that they're trying to pretend they're vampires or something. I seem to have stumbled into a bad re-enactment of *The Rocky Horror Picture Show*.

But I still don't understand how Sadie is managing to manipulate me. It *must* be a drug of some kind. I'll go along with it for now and try to get more information.

She's looking at me carefully, as if to gauge how close I am to freaking out.

I smile encouragingly to show her that I won't. 'So you're

sort of like my mistress then?'

She nods. Wow, OK, she's a dominatrix. I gulp. Maybe that's why she's never around much at night. She's off whipping men in a dungeon somewhere. But I've had a poke through her wardrobe when she wasn't here. I found some leather skirts, but no catsuit, handcuffs, or whips or anything.

I plaster a fake smile on my face. 'OK! That makes so much more sense. And you can get me to stay here ... how exactly?'

She hitches a shoulder. 'You have my venom in your system. That acts like a sort of drug, I guess. So technically, I have turned you into an addict, if you want to be really picky about it. But I haven't given you enough to make you crave it yet, just enough to make you easier to manage.'

Great. This is all good information. All I need to do now is find out how she gets the 'venom' (if that's what she's calling it) into my system.

'And how do you administer it?' I ask casually. 'Through my food or ...?'

Sadie parts her lips and taps one of her eyeteeth and then the other. 'I bite you. With these.'

I almost chuckle but manage to stifle it in time, and she doesn't seem to notice. Bite me? Wow, she really is taking this pretend vampire thing to the limit. Next thing she'll be popping in a pair of fake fangs!

I need to compliment her on her 'biting ability'. I read somewhere in a crime novel that a victim should give the kidnapper compliments so they get an ego boost and therefore become complacent and let their guard down.

'You must be very good at it,' I say placatingly. 'I haven't felt a thing.'

'Thanks, years of practice.'

'Oh, like how many years?'

Sadie tilts her head and considers. *This should be good*, I think.

'Two hundred and twenty-five,' she says with a smile. 'As I said, years of practice.'

The hairs on the back of my neck rise. That's a bit creepy and kind of authentic sounding. But I haven't seen anything equating to bite marks on my body when I've been washing it in the shower. I noticed I was losing a little muscle tone since I've been held captive, but I've since been doing some press-ups and sit-ups and leg lifts to counteract that. Also some jogging on the spot. I need to keep up my strength in case I need to fight off and outrun three women. Plus call me vain, but I've worked hard for these abs lugging equipment around, and I don't want to get pudgy.

'At least tell me about why you're keeping me here. I deserve to know. But don't give me any "I'm a vampire" bullshit because I won't believe it.'

Sadie is motionless, then slowly turns her head to face me. 'What would it take for you to believe it?' she asks.

I shrug. 'Uh, I dunno. Can you read my mind?'

She shakes her head. 'No, you're an anomaly in that respect.'

I smirk to myself. *Nice save. That lets you off the hook for telepathy.*

'Can you shape-shift into a bat?'

She shakes her head. 'No.'

'Eject mist from your pores?'

'No.'

'Fly?'

'No. Floss can, but not me.'

'Wow, that would be cool,' I say, going along with it. *Fly? Yeah right!* 'Shame you can't do that.'

Sadie narrows her eyes. 'You're starting to make me feel like a subpar vampire, Elliott.'

'Well, what *can* you do?' I say, poking her shoulder with my finger. When she doesn't respond, I poke her again.

'Don't niggle me, Elliott. I've been good about not messing with you. But if you push me, I will,' she asserts in a low threatening tone.

I can't help it. I laugh out loud. It just sounds so ridiculous! I'm taller and brawnier than her, and if she thinks she can overpower *me*, she really is nuts. I flex one of my biceps, which is toning up again nicely.

'I'd like to see you try,' I say confidently.

One second, I'm sitting on the bed; the next, I'm slammed against the wall above the headboard with so much force all the breath is expelled from my lungs.

Sadie stands on the bed below me, lightly bouncing, a look of concentration on her face.

'Urrrgghh,' I gasp as an unseen fist closes around my throat, cutting off most of my airway, but not quite. I can't move a muscle. It's like being flattened by an ironing board.

There's a sharp knock on the door. 'Sadie, what are you doing in there? You're not drinking from Elliott, are you?' It sounds like that Hester woman.

'No,' Sadie replies. 'We're just playing a little game.' With a smirk, she shifts me along the wall and back again, then up and down like I'm a Pac-Man.

'Oh, right. Well, keep the noise down.'

The invisible force releases me, and I fall onto the bed in a heap, gasping for breath. I clutch at Sadie's bare ankles, and she leans down and pats my head gently, as if I'm her pet.

'Believe me now, pretty boy?'

Chapter 20

Elliott | Highlands, present day

Talking to that thrall woman was like trying to get blood out of a stone. But I've deduced that, as there are 'many' of them, Alexander has reinvented himself as an immortal Hugh Hefner, God rest his smutty soul.

So where do I come into it? Why keep me alive? Surely, it's more hassle than it's worth?

The vague answers to those questions comes shortly after I've eaten my canned stew, and as it didn't agree with me, I had to manoeuvre onto the bucket and take a shit. (That's something I don't want to repeat in a hurry since now I have to lie here, smelling it.)

I start howling for help, hoping that someone hears me out the barred window. But knowing my luck, it probably leads to an open field, and the only things nearby are sheep. Five minutes later, the door creaks open, and Alexander strides in. My lips are instantly glued together mid-yell, and I can't speak. 'Mmmm mmmmm mmmm.'

'Yes, that's what happens, Elliott, when you're being too loud. It's giving me a headache. Do you promise not to shout anymore?' His voice is calm, but forceful, and his vampiric presence is powerful. I know he could end me quite easily, so I need to play docile.

I nod, and my lips are released. I take in deep lungfuls of air and get a proper look at my captor for the first time. I didn't have much of a chance last night as I was out of it from his feeding. So this is the famous Dr Alexander Dryden that Sadie and her flatmates have been hiding from for over a century.

The only description I've been given is that he's tall, dark, handsome, and has sharp fangs. Not exactly much to go on when you're trying to avoid being drained. Floss tried to do a sketch of him once for me. But—and I say this with utmost respect for her myriad abilities—she can't draw for shit. The end product looked like the Count from *Sesame Street*. Then she got scared that the drawing might inadvertently conjure him, and she had to rip it up. She's quite superstitious that way.

But now I have the real version standing in front of me. He's wearing a red silk robe, black silk pyjamas, a cravat, and black leather sheepskin slippers. His skin is white, and his features are pointy, giving him a rat-like appearance. His hair is black and slicked back with some grey threads, and his goatee beard is also touched with grey. I wouldn't call him 'handsome' personally. But I can see the silver fox appeal. It's just a pity that he set his sights on Floss when she turned up for that governess interview. If she'd been in her right mind, I'm sure she would've easily resisted his charms and gone for someone her own age. Damian is a much better choice than this undead fuckwit.

I haul myself upright against the wall, wincing as my bones creak and the iron cuff scrapes against my raw skin. Alexander ventures partway into the room but stops in his tracks and wrinkles his nose. He shakes his head disparagingly. 'What a terrible pong you've made, Elliott,' he drawls.

'Well, if you're going to feed me crappy stew,' I reply tightly. 'Be thankful I had a bucket. Otherwise, your posh slippers would be covered in shit.'

He grimaces at that and clicks his tongue. 'I'll get Lucy to empty it.' His eyes glaze over, and I assume he's summoning her to come and fetch my bucket. Poor thing. She gets all the good jobs.

'She needs a decent meal,' I remark, unable to help myself. 'What have you been doing to her?'

Alexander tilts his head, regarding me with unblinking brown eyes. 'What I do with my girls is no concern of yours.'

But as per usual, I can't keep my mouth shut. Not when someone's so obviously being maltreated.

'So what's the deal? Are you running a Playboy Thrall Mansion here or something?'

Alexander smirks. 'The less you know, the better.'

'So you're not going to tell me why I'm here?'

'Nope. But I will be requiring some more of your blood.'

I tense, thinking he's going to feed from me again, and I really don't want *that* to happen. I'm used to it, of course, with Sadie. But she drinks sustainably with one eye on my well-being. OK, if I'm being completely honest, sometimes she gets a bit carried away. But she always gives me a revitalising coffee and biscuits afterwards. Alexander took far too much last night, and I'm still recovering.

But instead of baring his fangs, he whips out a syringe from his robe pocket and advances towards me. I summon my energy, ready to give him a few well-aimed punches. But before I can raise my fist, a feeling of calm washes over me, and it drops to my side. I watch helplessly as he crouches beside me and sticks the crook of my arm with the needle, drawing up a vial of crimson blood.

When it's done, he places a thumb over the pinprick, applying pressure for thirty seconds or so. He lifts his bloodied thumb to his mouth and sucks it, grinning at me.

'Mmm, tasty. I can see why your girlfriend keeps you

around.'

'She's not my—'

'Ah, Lucy,' says Alexander without turning. 'Please empty and clean Elliott's bucket. That canned stew didn't agree with him. Give him spaghetti instead.'

Oh, yummy.

'Yes, Master,' she intones and shuffles forward to dutifully collect the bucket. To give her credit, she doesn't gag, but her nostrils flare at the smell.

'Sorry!' I mouth, and she nods and shuffles out after Alexander, who has placed the syringe back in his pocket.

The door clangs shut behind them.

Chapter 21

Sadie | London, 1758

Darius walks towards the bed, and I can't tear my eyes away from the monstrous bulge in his breeches. But now I'm confused by his intentions, and my burnt fingers are throbbing unbearably. I should have just climaxed from him licking me and taken the punishment rather than the prize. Because if the prize isn't him, then I don't want it.

From his pocket, he extracts a black silk scarf and ties it round my eyes, and I whimper as my world becomes dark. 'Shhh, be calm. She'll be here momentarily.'

I tense at that. *She?* 'Who?' I ask warily.

'The Mistress. Then the fun will really begin.' From the excited, feverish edge to his tone, my instincts tell me that the prize is definitely not within the realms of what I'm normally used to in bed. Oh hell's bells, is this going to turn into a threesome? I'm more of a one-to-one girl. This is not good! I attempt to free myself from whatever's holding me fast, but it's no use. I'm a sacrificial goat.

Quick footsteps tap on the floorboards outside the room, and Darius hastens to open the door. A pause and someone steps lightly into the room. There's a swish of material, as if a cloak is being removed, and a waft of frosty outside air feathers my cheek.

'Greetings, Mistress,' Darius says eagerly.

'Why are you still standing?' purrs an imperious female voice. 'You know I prefer you on your knees when you greet me. But at least you have removed your shirt. Good ... Now kneel before me.'

There's a soft thump, which I assume is Darius kneeling. 'I humbly apologise, Mistress,' he says, sounding like a breathless schoolboy. 'And I thank you for your gracious touch.'

The sound of a hand slapping hard against skin reaches my ears, and my eyebrows shoot up. *Is she punishing him? How? And why is he letting her?*

Whoever this woman is, she's got Darius Vexley tied around her little finger with a pink ribbon. I'm a bit green-eyed about that! I wish I had that kind of command and control over him. Or any man, for that matter. Her voice, manner, and actions are creating a powerful yearning in my gut to be called Mistress. But it's something I know can never be mine without birthright and breeding.

'And what of my evening's entertainment?' she says huskily once Darius has been thoroughly dealt with. An atmosphere of sexual tension now permeates the room, as if they both enjoyed the slapping. Some of the other girls at Mother Swift's take on customers who wish to engage in that kind of activity, and I often hear their distant screams rending the air as I service my own. It always makes me shudder and feel lucky I'm not them. But to be called Mistress, it seems I would need the stomach for doling out slaps.

'She is prepared, Mistress,' Darius replies. 'Ready and waiting for you on the bed. I tested her ... resolve ... and found her able to withstand my ministrations.'

There's a pause, and I sense unseen eyes raking my naked flesh. 'Excellent. Thank you, Darius. It bodes well. Unlike that other harlot you found for me who lasted barely five minutes.'

'Yes, Mistress.' Darius sounds regretful. 'But I have been watching this one for weeks. Her name is Sadie Smith ...'

I stiffen in surprise at that. *Watching me? Spying on me?*

'And she is in high demand from a number of elite gentlemen. Upon interviewing them, it was made clear to me that she only considers their pleasure and not her own. She is a perfect candidate for your purposes.'

A hoarse cackle of delight ensues, then a sniffing noise.

'But why can I smell burning flesh?'

Darius sighs. 'There was a slight ... incident. With the fire. I apologise. But other than that, she is untarnished. And it will heal when you—'

'Thank you, Darius. You can leave us now.'

'I was hoping I could ...' he trails off.

'Join in?' The woman sounds amused. 'Hmm, I don't know about that.'

'Oh please, let me,' Darius implores. To my ears, he sounds like he's practically begging. And from that huge erection I witnessed earlier, I'm not surprised he's frothing at the mouth for release.

'Very well. I can see that cock of yours is about to burst some buttons,' she says dryly.

I snigger at her shared response. 'My thoughts exactly!' I call over, unable to resist butting in.

There's a heavy silence, then a swish of material as the woman makes her way over to me on the bed. She stands there, saying nothing; and again, I sense eyes creeping over my body. I'm used to being naked, so it doesn't bother me. And I suppose I can help her out if she wants her own release, though I don't do women as a rule. It's Darius I'm more interested in. The scent of roses tickles my nose. It's the same scent that I smelled on Darius when he escorted me into the room. They must use the same rose water cologne or something. Are they friends? Lovers? The way she speaks to him suggests something else, more like master and slave.

'What is your name please, ma'am?' I ask, straining to see through the black silk mask but seeing nothing but the outline of a shadowy form beside the bed.

'You may call me ... Anya,' says the woman. A cool finger touches my burned hand, and I flinch. There's a tutting noise.

Did you do this to yourself?

For a moment, I'm confused, thinking she's spoken. But then I realise that I'm hearing her voice in my mind. How odd.

'Y-yes?'

Darius pushed you to your limits, little one, and this is what you chose instead of letting him win.

It's not a question, but I nod uncertainly anyway.

There's that hoarse cackling laugh again. *For that, and that alone, I think you and I will get along beautifully. But I sense confusion in you. Is there anything you wish to know?*

'Ah, well, now that you mention it. I was expecting to, excuse my French, fuck him over there.' I nod in the direction of Darius. 'But it appears that it is *you* who require my services?'

Indeed. The same cool finger trails along the soft underside of my breast, and I shiver. *Is that something you can help me with?*

I shrug. 'It's all the same to me, ma'am. A cunny's as good as a cock, as long as you can pay up. That's my one non-negotiable.'

The icy finger lightly circles my nipple, and my thighs

quiver. I swallow. She has got a lovely touch; and now I'm getting horny, imagining how nice her cold fingers will feel slipping around in my hot, wet cunny.

Oh, I can pay, and I will pay you well. Do you want me to put the money on the dresser now, little one?

I nod. 'Yes, please.' This is a very strange one-sided conversation I'm having, but the soft *thwip* of a drawstring purse opening and the clink of many coins being set up one by one is music to my ears. Despite the raid, my burnt fingers, being pinned to a bed and blindfolded, this night is turning out to be quite financially rewarding!

A minute later, there's a rustle as a dress falls to the ground; and Darius gives a low murmur of appreciation from the fireside, where I assume he's set himself up for a ringside seat. From his reaction, Anya—if that's her real name—is obviously the owner of a beautiful body. Is she connected to royalty or married to someone high up in society? Hence my mask? Is she worried that I might give her sapphic secret away? Or blackmail her?

Those are questions that I may never find out the answers to. The side of the bed dips, and Anya's marble-cold body slides against mine. Then the night that changes my life really begins.

CHAPTER 22

Sadie | Highlands, present day

It's raining heavily as we pull up outside Tim's cabin. I say 'cabin'; but the car lights illuminate a large architecturally designed home made of stone, wood, and solar panels bordered by a thicket of pine trees.

'Cool place,' says Floss, peering at it through the windscreen wipers.

'Yeah,' says Damian. 'Uncle Tim built it about ten years ago, and it's even won a sustainable home award. Well, I guess we should go and rouse the hermit.'

He switches off the car engine and lights. The house and surroundings are still easily visible with my night vision, though. As I get out of the car, my sensitive ears pick up the sound of rushing water nearby. And the rain-drenched air smells cold, fresh, and sweet. It's a lovely peaceful spot.

My stomach flips nervously. I'm not at all prepared for this meeting. The last time I saw Tim, he was in an apron cooking coq au vin at his kitchen stove, my arms were full of his cast-offs, and he was *not* happy with me. We sold up and moved to a more university-oriented part of town a couple of months after that because we came up with the idea of using students for blood donors. By that time, Elliott was completely in my thrall and fully on board with our plan. I didn't really give Tim another thought because I was too busy organising things. He has crossed my mind a few times over the years, though, typically along the lines of 'I wonder if he ever got married'. The fact that he lives alone in an off-grid cabin in the Highlands suggests that he didn't. Unless he's divorced. I could have checked up on him, I suppose, but I prefer to let sleeping dogs lie.

It's crazy that out of all the people in Edinburgh, Floss had to go and hook up with Tim's nephew. If I believed in karma, I'd say it was destiny that we were supposed to meet again because we have unfinished business. But I don't believe in that. I don't believe in anything.

We gather silently in front of a wide wooden door, which has an overhang from the roof protecting us from the rain. A gold tubular wind chime tinkles above, whipping around in the gusts from the storm. I hide behind Hester, easy to do because she's so tall.

Are you freaking out right now? she asks me.

Yeah, I admit, wiping drips from my face and smoothing my damp hair nervously. *I don't know how he's going to react when he sees me.*

Damian rings the doorbell, and there's no movement from inside. Then I detect a subtle thump of footsteps moving towards the entrance. Hester tilts her head, hearing them too.

Looks like you're going to find out in exactly three, two ...

'Damian. What are you doing here?'

I shut my eyes, resting my forehead against Hester's back, as a mixture of regret and nostalgia washes over me at hearing Tim's surprised, but familiar voice. I tend to put on a staunch facade, but only because underneath I'm such a fucking coward when it comes to emotional entanglements.

'Hey, Tim. Uh, we're just passing through. I know it's a bit short notice, but would you be able to put us up for the night? I would have rung ahead, but Dad said you're completely off-grid now.'

'Yes, of course. Come in, come in.' From his even tone, I assume it's too dark for him to have had a good look at Damian's *friends.*

But at least he said 'come in'! That makes things easier.

We all shuffle past into a grey slate tiled foyer, where the light is brighter, and I risk a peek at Tim standing aside to let us in.

Shit, he's still good-looking. Older, of course. But he has

all his hair and a beard too, salt-and-pepper coloured. And he's in great shape. His arms are brawny, and his khaki long-sleeved T-shirt is tight across his chest. Camel corduroy trousers cover muscular thighs. He looks like a mountain man. He must chop wood or go for long country walks or something.

'So what brings you ...' he starts saying, then catches sight of Floss. His eyes widen, then drop to her and Damian's clasped hands.

'You may have met my girlfriend, Floss, before,' says Damian calmly. 'And her flatmates.'

'Hi, Tim,' says Floss casually, and Hester nods at him.

It's time I made an appearance. *Now or never*, I think.

Popping out from behind her, I do jazz hands. 'Surprise!'

It's meant to be funny, but the look of shock on Tim's face and the way he staggers back when he sees me suggest that it doesn't land too well.

'Sadie. What the ...' he gasps, pressing a hand to his chest.

Yikes, I hope he's not going to have a heart attack, I think to the others. *Quick, someone relax him.*

I could do it, but it feels too intimate to be pacifying my ex-boyfriend.

On it, says Floss, *since he's kind of my uncle now too.*

Floss works her soothing magic, and Tim's facial muscles

slacken into a drowsy smile.

***

'Your house is incredible,' I say, gazing at the soaring vaulted ceiling, chunky grey stone fireplace, and polished concrete floors. The lounge is austere but softened by faux fur animal rugs, various artworks on the walls, and a fawn velvet couch, which I'm now sitting on with Tim.

'Did you design it yourself?'

'Thank you. Yes, with a little help from one of my architect friends.'

Tim takes a sip of chamomile tea and settles back beside me. I have a cup steaming on the glass coffee table too, and I've taken a couple of polite sips.

The others have vanished to their guest rooms, with the excuse of 'freshening up' before dinner, leaving us alone. Tim mentioned that he'd throw something together in a bit. I know he and Damian need to eat, but I'm not quite sure how the rest of us are going to get around that aspect. I had a private conversation with Hester while Tim was making the tea.

Me: *What are we going to do about dinner?*

Hester: *We'll have to pick at it. It's either that or go out hunting tonight for an animal. We should probably keep our blood bags for emergency backup in case we need it. They should be OK in the car boot.*

Me: Good idea. Hopefully, whatever Tim cooks, it's meat-based. If it's tofu, I'm not touching it.

Hester: Me neither!

Knowing Floss and Damian, they'll probably have one of their special 'naps', and she'll feed from him. It makes me crave Elliott just thinking about it. I miss his blood, his scent. Him. But I can't start falling apart now. I've still got to endure another hypnosis session, and I need to stay strong and positive so we can find him.

'It's really great to see you,' says Tim as I drift off, staring into the insipid yellow tea, thinking about Elliott, and hoping wherever he is, someone's looking after him.

'Huh? Oh, you too.' I run a critical eye over him again, noting the way his bicep flexes as he drinks his tea. 'Don't take this the wrong way, but you look great for your age.'

He huffs a laugh. 'I have a home gym. Keeps me out of trouble.'

'So you work in ...?'

'Tech start-ups. I invest early, then cash out.'

'Nice.'

'Yeah, it's high-risk, but high reward.'

'Still, you must be doing all right to afford this.' I indicate the room with my chin.

He shrugs. 'I built this from the nest egg I'd put aside for our future. After thirty years, I finally got over you. So I decided to get out of Edinburgh and use the money. And here you are, looking pretty much exactly like the Sadie standing in my kitchen the day we broke up. Different hair'—he reaches out and briefly touches my cheek—'but same beautiful face.'

We lock eyes, my light blue to his dark blue; and I feel a gentle tug on my cold, desiccated heart—just a small one, not enough to kick-start it or anything. But Tim and I *were* good together at the beginning. We had fun. Until he started getting too serious. Like now. I mean, what is he talking about? Thirty years to get over me. That can't be right.

I lick my lips nervously and shift along the couch a little.

'But surely, you've had other relationships since me?'

'Not really. No one ever compared to you, my mysterious Sadie. There was always something different about you. It's why I fell in love with you ... *am* still in love with you.'

I puff out my cheeks, digesting this. Fuck. I knew it was a bad idea to come here. It's *my* fault Tim's turned into an off-grid hermit. Even worse, this amazing house was built with money *meant for us* and possibly where I would be living now if I'd ended up marrying him.

'Of course, I had my suspicions back then that you weren't completely ... human,' he continues.

'Did you?' I sip my tea, glad that he's bringing up the subject finally. Ugh, this tea is foul. What I really need is something more nutritious. I eye Tim's tanned firm neck with only the barest trace of sagging skin. Now if I could get my fangs into that for a minute …

'Yeah, I woke up one night to discover you feeding from me. At the time, when I told my brother you might be a vampire, Malcolm said I was being ridiculous. But seeing you here now, looking like a fresh-faced twenty-something, it confirms I was right all along. It's a consolation that I wasn't crazy at least.'

'Why didn't you say something?' I ask incredulously.

'I didn't know how to broach the subject. Didn't want to drive you away. In the end, I did anyway.'

'It wasn't your fault.'

Tim takes the cup from me and places it on the glass coffee table. He grasps my cold hands in his warm ones. 'No, Sadie. I should have fought harder for you that day,' he says earnestly. 'I was angry. I'm sorry. I thought it best to let things cool off, but I waited too long. By the time I went to contact you, to see if you wanted to give it another go, your flat had different owners.' He shakes his head. 'That was a bad day.'

I extract one of my hands and place it on the back of his. 'Don't worry, it's all in the past now,' I say gently. Perhaps I should wipe his memory of this visit, if it's too hard seeing me again.

'Is it, though?' he insists. 'I still feel the same.'

I pat his hand idly. 'Tim, be reasonable. You know what I am. It could never work.' *And besides, there's Elliott.* But I don't mention him. Tim is obviously a bit nuts, and he might crack completely if he knows there's another man in the picture.

'Yes, I know what you are,' he says patiently. 'But I don't care. I'm sick of living in limbo without you. I want you to do what I should've asked you to do in the first place.'

'What's that?' I ask nervously.

Tim smiles. 'Turn me, of course, so we can be together again.'

CHAPTER 23

Elliott | Highlands, present day

Lucy returns with my clean bucket and places it on the floor next to me.

'Really sorry about that,' I apologise again. I hope she had some rubber gloves at least, but as her hands are dripping wet and glowing pink with cold, it looks like that's a no.

She nods, straightens, and heads towards the door.

Growing desperate about my future well-being, I attempt to override her enthralled state.

'Lucy, look at me!'

She jerks around, her eyes meeting mine. Even if they're glazed and distant, that's a good start.

'If you help me escape, I have friends—vampire friends— who will protect you. You don't have to live like this,' I say in a low urgent tone.

Lucy hitches a shoulder. 'I can't.' She sounds mournful.

'You can, and you will,' I state firmly. 'You *will* help

me.'

She takes a step backwards. 'No, Master will be angry. He needs your blood.'

My ears perk up at that.

'Why? Why does he need my blood?'

She shakes her head. 'I don't know.'

'You do know.'

'I don't.'

'Lucy, please, please, *please* listen to me!'

But she stands there, looking vacant. Wow, he's really messed with her brain. What a prick.

I rattle my chain to get her attention. The noise seems to rouse her. For a second, her eyes clear, and she looks right at me.

'Yes, Lucy. You can do this. Get me out of here.'

She nods slowly. And for a second, I feel supremely hopeful that I'm going to be freed.

Then her eyes cloud over again, and she turns and runs out the door. It clangs shut behind her.

***

The day drags on. Morning turns to afternoon. Shadows shift and move along the walls. Bored and exhausted from all the bloodletting and lack of decent food, I nod off.

A scuffling noise jerks me awake, and I open my eyes to find Alexander crouching over me. Something glints in the gloom, and I look down to find he has a syringe in his hand.

He sticks the thin needle in my arm and starts drawing out another vial of blood.

'Noooo! Leave me alone!' I moan and try to pull away.

'Can't do that, I'm afraid,' he says, holding my arm steady until the vial is full. He places his thumb over the wound like before. My mouth is so dry that my tongue feels too big for it.

'Water,' I rasp weakly.

'I'll get Maya to bring you some,' he replies, licking his thumb. 'Can't have you shrivelling up like a prune. You're too important for that.'

'Don't you mean Lucy?' I mumble.

But Alexander doesn't say anything. Just leaves me lying there surrounded by straw, feeling weak and confused. It begs the question if I'm so important, why aren't I being looked after better? Surely, I deserve a proper room in his Playboy Thrall Mansion? Maybe I'll demand that next time he takes blood from me.

Shortly afterwards, a young woman enters, bearing a lamp and a plastic jug of water. She has red hair and is slightly less thin than Lucy, but still not healthy. Her eyes are round and haunted-looking. This must be Maya.

'Thank you,' I say when she places the jug by the bucket. She doesn't reply. I lift the jug to my lips and gulp down some mouthfuls of ice-cold water gratefully.

'Where's Lucy?' I ask, now worrying that something has happened to her. 'Is she OK?'

Again, no reply. The woman backs away towards the door, but in the lamplight, I can see my questions have rattled her. And her eyes are shiny, like they're filling with tears.

A clang of the door and I'm alone again.

I drink some more water, trying to remain positive. But it's difficult not to be afraid. Something has obviously happened to Lucy, and I'm starting to think this is curtains for me too. That I'm going to cark it in this dungeon, and I'm never going to see Sadie again.

CHAPTER 24

Sadie | Highlands, present day

For the first time in my long life, I have no idea what to say. I stare at Tim's smiling face, bewildered. He wants me to turn him? And he's happy about that? Going off-grid has really made him lose the plot.

Someone behind us clears their throat and thankfully interrupts the moment. I yank my hands away from Tim's and glance around to find Damian standing there, looking at us curiously.

'It's getting on. We should do that hypnosis session, Sadie,' he says.

Tim looks from him to me. 'Hypnosis?'

'Long story. We're trying to find someone,' I explain.

Tim raises an eyebrow but doesn't ask questions. 'I need to start on dinner anyway. Is there anything you'd like …?'

'Meat, rare,' I say promptly.

He nods. 'I can do that.'

It's weird how quickly Tim has adjusted to me being a

vampire. He's not reacting how I would expect him to. Maybe he's sick of being human or just really bored living in the country and needs some excitement.

'What's going on with you two?' Damian enquires as I follow him up a short flight of stairs to the first floor landing, where a tall narrow window looks out onto the darkened forest.

'Nothing.'

'Didn't look like nothing to me. You were holding hands,' he states mock accusingly.

I sigh. 'There's a slight complication. Your uncle is still in love with me and wants me to turn him.'

Damian gives a short laugh.

'It's not funny!'

'It kind of is under the circumstances. Are you going to?'

'Of course not! If I'm going to turn anyone, it would be Elliott.' I stare at the back of his vulnerable neck. 'But I am feeling a little hungry, and you did promise I could feed on you, remember?'

Damian pauses on the stair above me, and I hear him swallow.

'Uh, yeah. But maybe after you've had dinner.'

When we're in his room, I settle on the bed, and he pulls up a chair. The bedcovers are rumpled, so I assume Floss has had a feeding session from Damian, and she's feeling nice and satiated. Lucky cow. She's currently next door with Hester, helping her learn her lines for her *Twelfth Night* audition. I hope she gets it. Seeing Hester act in a play would be quite amusing, and of course, we should go to London with her for moral support. After we rescue Elliott, of course. It's going to happen. The buzzing in my brain is steady and comforting, letting me know he's still with us. Still alive.

'OK, Sadie. It's the same process as before. Relax and clear your mind. I'll count backwards and take you under.'

I nod and close my eyes. Damian does his hypnosis spiel in a calm, steady voice and starts counting down. One minute, I'm looking at darkness. The next, an inner eye opens; and suddenly, I'm looking at a different room.

'What can you see?'

'It's kind of dark, but I can make out stone walls.'

'Great, Sadie,' says Damian. 'Anything in particular about the room that you notice?'

I strain to see. But I'm dependent on Elliott's limited human vision since I'm perched in his head. 'Straw on the ground. A stone floor. A bucket. Sorry, that's not much help.'

'OK. It sounds like he's lying in some kind of cell, maybe a dungeon?'

I nod. 'Yes, that feels right.'

'Concentrate on how he feels. What sort of physical state is he in?'

'Tired. Hangry. Missing me.' I bite my lip, a bit upset at that.

'Go on, it's OK.'

'He doesn't know what's happening. Or where he is. Only that Alexander has been drawing blood from him with a syringe.'

'Interesting.'

'Yeah.'

I stiffen as a shadow crosses my vision. 'Someone's there with him.'

'Who is it? Friend or foe?'

'Not sure. But Elliott's trying to move away from them. He's afraid.'

The figure lunges at him, and I feel Elliott's shock, my hands instinctively clutching for him. 'Oh no! Someone's attacking him, and he's defenceless!'

With a growl, I launch myself at Elliott's attacker and sink my fangs into their neck. I'm going to drain them. How dare they touch my thrall!

No, Sadie! Damian gasps in my head. *Don't!*

But all I can think about is protecting Elliott. *I must.* I take several long pulls, the spurt of warm liquid in my mouth goading me to take more. Elliott lets out a groan, or is it Damian? I'm not sure anymore as, by now, I'm crazed and confused by bloodlust. *Don't worry, Elliott, I'll save you this time!* I yell, pinning the unseen attacker to the ground and taking my fill.

Sadie, please. Damian's voice filters weakly through the red mist, and I wonder briefly why he isn't bringing me out of the hypnosis. No matter. I drink some more.

There's a piercing scream, and I'm flung across the cell, hitting the stone wall with a thump. Everything goes black.

When I come to, I'm not lying on the bed. I'm on the other side of the room, and Floss and Hester are there, huddled together. Floss is whimpering.

'What's going on?' I ask groggily.

'Stay over there!' hisses Hester. 'You've done enough!'

What have I done? I don't remember. There's something sticky on my chin, a delicious taste in my throat. I swallow and move my tongue around, licking at my lips. *Mmm, blood. How did that get there?* I wonder.

Hester: *You nearly drained Damian! He's not doing well. Floss had already drunk from him. His pulse is really weak.*

Me: *What?*

I crawl over to them on my hands and knees. Nudging them aside, I stare at Damian lying prostrate on the floor.

His eyes are closed, and his face is grey. There are two bloodied holes in his neck.

Shit, did I do that? I ask the others.

Floss: *Yes! Why the* fuck *did you bite him?*

Me: *I was under hypnosis. I didn't mean to! And wow, I can hear you loud and clear.*

This is the first time she's been able to project her thoughts to me. I'm impressed.

Floss: *Never mind that. What are we going to do?*

Me: *Calm down. Just turn him. Job done.*

Floss: *But he hadn't decided yet!*

I gaze down at Damian's fluttering eyelids and listen to his hoarse shallow breathing.

Me: *I guess I made that decision for him. But you're going to have to do it quickly. He's fading fast.*

Chapter 25

Elliott | Highlands, present day

There's someone or something in the cell with me. In the corner. Glinting eyes are watching me. Drawing in a shaky breath, I call out into the darkness, 'Who's there?' I try to sound as bold as I can, but the words catch in my throat.

Nails click on stone. The sound of licking.

Is it ... a cat? Has Alexander taken pity on me and thrust an emotional support pet in here to keep me company? But the dark shape moving towards me from the shadows is too large for a cat, even if I want to keep telling myself it is one.

'Nice kitty,' I choke out. 'There, there. You won't hurt me, will you?'

Nails click closer.

A squelching sound.

It's almost upon me before I see what it is.

My blood runs cold, and I piss myself a little.

'*Ohhh nooo*,' I moan. I'm dead. I'm sooooo dead.

It lunges for my neck.

* * *

It's strange. In my final moments, when all the life is being sucked from my body, I sense that Sadie is here too. That she pushes Lucy off me and tackles her to the ground. I distinctly hear her yelling, *Don't worry, Elliott, I'll save you this time!*

But it must be only wishful thinking. Wanting her to hold me and revitalise me, bring me back from the brink. Because I know when someone is taking too much, and with all the blood Alexander's been drawing, I'm at my limit faster than I would be.

Lucy's mouth, suckling hard at my neck, is giving me the sweet kiss of death. I hover on a mossy stone ledge, about to fall into a deep dark well. Then a bloodied wrist is thrust at my lips.

'Drink, Elliott,' Lucy commands. Her thin pale face is inches from my own, nose and chin smeared with my blood and the tips of her white fangs protruding. 'Drink now.'

I struggle to comprehend what's happening. Am I not about to die? Am I being given a gift? This is what I've been waiting for, for forty years. But it's not who I wanted it to be from!

Lucy frantically rubs her iron-tanged wrist over my mouth when I don't respond. 'Quickly!' she urges.

I can feel myself fading fast, and I know I don't have time to be precious about it. I want to be strong. I want to be a vampire. *I want to tell Sadie how I feel about her.*

Eagerly, I latch on to the wound in Lucy's wrist and begin guzzling her blood.

'That's it, Elliott,' she purrs, stroking my head. 'Take your fill from me. Choose immortal life.'

I groan, unable to drink any more, and slump back against the wall. Lucy's blood and venom sizzle like fire through my veins. It's a feeling I know well and why I'm so addicted to Sadie, but she gives me only a taster to keep me hooked. This is more intense, like something is physiologically rearranging inside of me. 'Now what?' I gasp.

My beautiful, yet ghastly saviour smiles as she gently strokes my stubbled cheek. 'Now we wait.'

Chapter 26

Sadie | London, 1758

Anya releases my wrists from the bonds (a relief as my arms were aching). *Touch me, little one. I want your hands on my body.*

Her voice resounds in my mind, and I feel like saying, 'I can't actually see your body due to this blasted blindfold.' But she isn't paying for my opinion, so I reach out, and my fingers touch cool smooth skin. Dutifully, I give several light strokes down her back and then over her breasts, which are as full and bouncy as ripe melons. Touching her doesn't stoke my own fire as much as I thought it would. But the fact that Darius is watching from the armchair and may be invited to join us at some point is giving me a sense of sensual anticipation.

Anya writhes around and arches her back even though I'm barely doing anything. This is going to be the easiest coin I've procured in a while. Perhaps I should extend my services to women in future?

That feels lovely. Now stroke between my legs.

Again, I'm compelled to do as she instructs. But the experience is strange. By that, I don't mean she doesn't have all the usual equipment down there, but her cunny is so icy! Like sticking my fingers into a slush pile of snow.

Oh yes, right there. Anya moans, jiggling her hips as I twiddle her sensitive nub.

Hmm, this talking in my head is very disconcerting, and the black silk mask is annoying me.

'I will remove this blindfold, Anya, ma'am,' I say, taking my hand from between her legs. 'I can pleasure you much better if I can see what I'm doing.'

I start to bring both hands up to my face, and Anya clicks her tongue. My hands are suddenly frozen in mid-air, and I can't move them in any direction, though I try with all my might. Fear clutches at my heart. Who is this woman that she can wield magic and speak in my head? Is she a witch?

'You are quite wilful, aren't you, little one?' Anya says, sounding amused. She tweaks at one of my nipples.

'My name is Sadie,' I reply, getting a bit tired of her calling me 'little one'. I clench my teeth and yank my hands, but they won't move an inch. 'Please free my hands.'

No, Sadie, she purrs, continuing her ministrations on my other nipple. *I don't trust that you won't remove the mask.*

'I won't, I promise,' I tell her truthfully.

But Anya simply *hmms* and licks slowly at the juncture between my neck and shoulder. Her tongue feels like a cold, wet slug lashing my heated skin. I'm not sure I like it. But I don't have much choice in the matter.

Eventually, after nuzzling and licking that spot on my neck for what seems like an age, Anya calls out sharply, 'Darius, come! Crawl to me!'

I rub my thighs together expectantly. Oooh, this is a better turn of events.

Darius utters a husky growl, and there's a soft thump and a slapping noise on the floorboards, as if he is indeed crawling over. Oh, how I wish I could see that! Darius crawling naked towards the bed with his big cock swinging between his legs.

I smile engagingly and angle my head in his direction, confident that he can help with two problems I'm having right now: my hands being locked in place and my cunny desperately wanting his attention.

'What is your bidding, Mistress?' he intones calmly, but as he's right next to the bed, I hear him swallow hard. He must be contemplating our naked bodies up close. Oh yes, Darius! Me first!

There's a pause, as if Anya's considering. 'You may attend to Sadie,' she says at last. 'She is aroused by the thought of your cock in her ... and I'm feeling generous tonight. So you can give her pleasure while I feed.'

I blink at that. Feed? Did she bring some bread and cheese with her? Is she going to eat it while watching us fuck? Well, she's paying, so whatever floats her boat!

'I would also like to ... feed,' says Darius, sounding hopeful. There's a distinct sound of him licking his lips.

I roll my eyes. So he'd rather have bread and cheese than give me a seeing-to. Charming!

Anya clicks her tongue again, this time in annoyance. 'You are being quite wilful too. There must be something in the air tonight. No, you cannot partake.'

'But I'm hungry ...' Darius whines.

'No,' says Anya firmly.

'But—' begs Darius.

'Silence!' commands Anya.

My head is rolling left and right on the pillow as their exchange goes on over me, my hands still frozen above me in mid-air.

'Er, apologies for interrupting, Anya,' I say. 'But I don't want to cause any trouble. I might return to Mother Swift's and leave you in peace to have your supper ...'

Anya barks that hoarse cackle of hers. 'Oh no, Sadie. You're not going anywhere.'

'I'm not?'

'No, little one. You *are* my supper.'

CHAPTER 27

Sadie | Highlands, present day

'Now, Floss, or he'll die!' I insist.

With a moan of despair, Floss holds out her wrist to me, and I puncture it with my fangs. She holds it over Damian's lips, and her blood drips into his mouth. He swallows feebly, and I feel reassured by that. 'That's good,' I tell her. 'If he can ingest enough, then the transition will start taking place.'

'Oh god,' says Floss, sounding freaked out. 'I'm turning him. I can't believe this is happening.'

'Didn't you talk about this with him?' asks Hester, kneeling on Damian's other side. 'He kind of knew it had to happen. Since Alexander threatened to kill you both.'

'Of course. But I didn't think I'd be doing it right now.' She closes her eyes and tilts her head back. 'I feel a bit sick. H-how is he doing?'

Hester feels for Damian's pulse. 'He's still alive, if that's what you mean. Not undead yet.'

Damian's face is a mottled grey, and his lips are tinged with blue. A stark contrast to the scarlet blood currently sliding through them. I watch from the sidelines in part horror, part fascination. I haven't seen many people transition before. I've been practising sustainable feeding for decades. And I'm super careful with Elliott, though he's been asking me to turn him for years.

'Sorry, Floss,' I say guiltily. I know she wanted to make it a romantic occasion for him with lighted candles, incense, his favourite music, etc. But realistically, what were the chances of that happening? I certainly never got that, and neither did the other two. She really does live in a fantasy world sometimes.

Floss ignores me. She wipes a trickle of blood oozing from the side of Damian's lips and cradles his head in her lap, rocking him. She starts crooning, 'Ladybird, ladybird, fly away home ...'

I shudder. Alexander sang that to her when she transitioned; it feels creepy somehow. 'You can stop singing that right now,' I say. 'If you want to sing him something rousing, try "Born This Way" by Lady Gaga.'

Hester snickers, and I throw her a grateful glance, glad to see that someone appreciates my sense of humour.

Damian's legs start twitching, his head lolls back, and the whites of his eyes show under his lids. He lets out a low moan.

'There you see, it's happening!' I exclaim, patting Floss on the arm with what I hope she takes as reassurance. I almost suggest I film it on my phone so they can watch it together later like a macabre wedding video.

Hmm, maybe not. But still—it's exciting!

***

Twenty minutes later, I'm not so sure that 'exciting' is the right word for it. Damian is certainly transitioning, but not in a good way. After his body spasming for a bit, he crawled off into the far corner and is now lying there groaning, and occasionally hiccuping.

Hester and I sit on the bed while Floss kneels near Damian, attempting to connect with him. 'Babe, are you OK? Babe, say something.' He only growls and whimpers like he's in pain. She stretches out her hand to touch his shoulder, but he snaps at it, and she hurriedly draws it back. His eyes are red and sore-looking, and his mouth is bunched up weirdly.

'Is this normal?' she whispers worriedly, looking over at us. 'I can't hear his thoughts or get him to respond to me at all.'

'Perfectly,' I say with a confidence I don't feel. 'Everyone transitions differently. He'll be fine.'

'Yes,' Hester agrees uncertainly. 'It's probably only teething issues. I'm sure he'll be hunky-dory in no time.'

Damian lets out a noise that sounds like fingernails scraping down a blackboard, and I scooch back behind Hester just in case he goes for us. Newbie vampires are unpredictable, and their bloodlust is at an all-time high. I vaguely recall my own experience; there were a lot of sore necks the following night!

Damian suddenly leaps into a crouching stand, his eyes are now neon-green and he has pale skin. His purple-streaked hair adds to the whole supernatural effect. He touches the tips of his white pointed teeth gingerly with his tongue, as if they're an equal source of pain and fascination.

He takes a step forward, baring them menacingly, and we all shrink back in fear.

Boo!

His voice comes through loud and clear in my mind, and from the looks of surprise on Floss's and Hester's faces, they heard it too.

Floss smiles with pride. *Aw, babe! That's great, you can talk to us! Say something else.*

Damian screws up his face in concentration. *Hungry. Eat. Now.*

Me: *OK, so we may have to wait a few months before we get more than baby talk …*

Damian snarls and licks his lips.

Me: *But you're doing really well!*

Telepathy came through for me straightaway too, so I'm betting some of my venom must have mixed in with Floss's, both from me biting Damian's neck and sinking my fangs into her wrist. It's not a pure transition, which is why he's been struggling. He's got a combination of powers attempting to come through. Interesting. Who knows what other ones he'll exhibit?

'He needs to feed,' says Hester aloud. 'That should take the edge off. Any volunteers?'

No one puts their hand up.

'We could take him into the forest and let him run around,' I suggest helpfully. 'I'm sure he'll catch an animal of some sort …'

'I don't know,' says Floss looking worried. 'A vampire on the loose sounds dangerous. What if he comes across some wild campers?'

'It's winter,' counters Hester. 'The chances of that happening are quite slim.'

'What about just giving him dinner then? Isn't Uncle Tim preparing raw meat?'

'Damian can't sit at the dinner table with his uncle, pretending nothing's wrong,' I say. 'Look at him!'

We stare at Damian, who is pacing to and fro in front of

us like a caged animal, venom dripping from his fangs.

'Sadie's right,' says Hester. 'He needs a proper drink. What about giving him the emergency blood?'

'Yes, isn't this an emergency?' agrees Floss.

'I'd rather keep that for us,' I say. 'I don't need an energy boost after my ... feed. But you two will, especially Floss after donating to Damian.'

They don't say anything in protest, but I sense their hunger. 'So we're all agreed?' I press. 'You guys grab a pick-me-up. Then we take him into the forest and let him stretch his vampy legs?'

The other two nod slowly.

Damian tilts his chin and sniffs the air sharply, as if he can smell his dinner already.

'I'm so sorry it turned out like this, babe,' Floss whispers.

'There's no time for that,' I say pragmatically. 'I'll go and talk to Tim and say something's come up—namely his nephew is now a vampire. I'll impress upon him the implications of that and why we need to exit the house asap.'

I might also suggest that he lock himself into his bedroom as well. If Damian catches a whiff of Tim's blood, there's no telling what he'll do. 'Going off-grid' might take on a whole new meaning.

CHAPTER 28

Elliott | Highlands, present day

Grasping the shackle around my wrist, I tear it away as if it were made of cardboard. I leap to my feet, curling my hands into fists, fangs extending through my gums. I'm going to make Alexander pay for upsetting Sadie and for keeping me locked up down here and using me for his sick science experiments.

As if she senses my intentions (and since she's now my sire, she probably can), Lucy grips my arm with surprising strength, effectively keeping me from striding towards the dungeon door.

'Don't, Elliott,' she murmurs.

I look down at her hand on my arm.

'Why shouldn't I? That fuck deserves to be drained after all the angst he's caused over the centuries. I'm sick of living my life looking over one shoulder in case he's lurking around.'

Lucy gives a giggle, and I frown, then realise what I've

said. Ah, right. Technically, I'm not *living* anymore. The transition was surprisingly easy, not nearly as bad as Sadie has been making out for all these years. I bounce lightly on the balls of my feet as renewed strength races through my muscles. I don't feel tired or hungry anymore. I feel like I could run a marathon. Scratch that. I feel like I could compete in a *triathlon.*

'Look, I know it's tempting. But trust me, you don't want to spend the first night of the rest of your immortal life with vampire blood on your hands.'

Hmm, Lucy is awfully chatty now that she's not under Alexander's thrall. But I suppose it makes sense. And I need to figure out how to get back to Sadie, who's probably worried sick about me.

I sigh and edge away from the wooden bucket, which, although clean, still emits the faint aroma of poo. My vampire nose is extra sensitive, something that surprises me. Even more, I can see in the dark, which is pretty cool. Lucy is standing before me surrounded by a purple light that picks out the shadows in her sunken cheeks.

'Plus I want to get back to my house and see if my cat is still alive. I've been stuck here for weeks,' she adds.

I relent and sweep my arm towards the door. 'Fine. Lead the way.'

'Gladly,' she says.

'What about your friends?' I ask, remembering it's not just us here. 'Should we rescue them too?'

She shakes her head sadly. 'Alexander keeps them all on a tight leash upstairs. There's no way we can break his enthrallment to get them out, not without endangering ourselves.'

Lucy opens the dungeon door with one finger as if it's as light as a feather, and we step through into a stone corridor bordered by a set of steps at one end. 'I'm confused,' I whisper. 'How did you become a vampire? Didn't Alexander turn you?'

'No, he didn't,' she whispers back. 'There's no time to explain. Let's get out of here first before he suspects anything's up. He's going to be furious when he discovers we're both missing, along with these ...' She pats the pocket of her skirt, which clinks softly, but I don't ask questions. For now, I want to be outside these castle walls, safe from danger, and revel in my new-found vampiric state. It's a goddamn miracle!

***

Lucy leads the way up the short flight of stairs, and we wind along a narrow corridor, which slopes upwards. At the end of this, she opens a studded wooden door. It creaks slightly;

and we tense, poised, her eyes raised to the stone ceiling above, listening for any movement. When none comes, she places a finger to her lips and motions for me to slip through the gap. It's such a relief to be out of that gloomy dungeon, and I'm so eager to escape that I hardly take any notice of my surroundings. Except for the fact that we're in a kitchen and the fittings are surprisingly modern. And there's a sign on the wall that says 'Home Sweet Home', which makes me want to laugh. I'm starting to think this is a Scottish retreat that Alexander has booked on Airbnb. I'll have to pump Lucy for more information once we're outside.

Speaking of pumping, I'm also very aware that my cock is hard and quite interested in following closely behind Lucy, even though she isn't wearing the saucy French maid's outfit anymore, but jeans and a top. I'm going to have to be on my guard as she's a new vampire too, and no doubt she's feeling as intensely horny as I am. I have nothing against undead sex per se, but I don't want to do it with her. I want my first time as a vampire to be with Sadie, the woman I—

'This way, Elliott,' Lucy whispers. Before I can react, she forcibly pulls me through a side door, and we pop out into cold fragrant night air peppered with the scent of pine. It's been raining, and I can smell wet earth and the herby scent of grass. Above us, a cluster of silver stars twinkles in the black velvet sky, and I detect the sharp metallic scent of ozone.

A door clangs somewhere inside the castle, and we freeze. Lucy gently closes the kitchen door and locks it silently with an iron key.

'Run!' she hisses and sprints off into the nearby undergrowth. The castle appears to be surrounded by dense forest on one side, which is an excellent hiding spot. Alexander will never find us in here.

Resisting the urge to whoop, I bound off after Lucy, easily keeping her in sight as she whips through the violet trees, my footfalls deadened by leaf litter. This is fun! I wish Sadie were here so we could run through the forest like fawns together. But knowing her, she'd complain heartily if she was wearing stilettos.

Lucy skids to a stop in front of a wide tree with a wizened, twisted trunk, and I almost barrel into her.

'Wha ...?'

'Shhh, can you hear that?'

I listen and detect the faint sound of something crashing through the undergrowth. It sounds quite far away, though. 'Alexander?' I whisper.

She shakes her head. 'Wrong direction. Unless he's circled around us.'

'We should keep moving away from that sound then. Try

and find a road ... or a village.'

Lucy gives me a slight smirk, a fang skimming her lower lip.

'Perhaps we should feed before we go gatecrashing a village?'

As soon as she says that, underneath the adrenaline flooding my system, I become aware of a persistent gnawing ache to satiate my thirst too. Lucy inches closer to me, and I swallow, closing my eyes. Thinking only of Sadie. And her beautiful pale throat. She's mine. I want to claim her with a fierceness that shakes my unholy body to its core.

Lucy reaches for my throat, her fangs bared, and I instinctively hold up my wrist for her to latch on to. 'Sorry, you'll have to make do with this instead.'

She pouts, but her feeding from my neck feels too intimate. We hardly know each other, and I'm not giving up my vampire virginity to her willingly.

However, that doesn't stop Lucy from trying to grab my cock while she feeds from my wrist.

'Stop that,' I say sternly, whisking my hips to the right and left like I'm in *Dirty Dancing* so she can't get hold of it.

'But you're so hot, and I'm so horny,' she whines. 'We could have a quickie here against the tree—'

'I have a girlfriend,' I explain hurriedly as my cock begins engorging when presented with that idea. Down, boy!

I don't blame Lucy. I know she has newbie vampire needs, and I do too; images of us rolling around on the forest floor naked are currently flooding my brain. I give myself a hard mental shake. *Yes, it would be easy*, I think. *We could satisfy our bloodlust urges right here and now.*

But the thought of having to confess to Sadie when I do eventually make it back to Edinburgh stops me. With an effort, I wrench my wrist from Lucy's mouth and push her away. Her face falls, and I feel like a prick.

'I'm really sorry. I'm just ... taken.'

Chapter 29

Sadie | Highlands, present day

Thanks to vampirism, all three of us are fast runners. It comes with the territory. But Damian's going at double superhuman speed. He zips along the forest trail like lightning, and we're barely able to keep up with him.

Me: *Jesus, we'll reach Glencoe if he carries on like this!*

Floss: *Keep him in sight. Hopefully, he'll slow down soon!*

As the fastest, Floss's slightly ahead, her long dark hair rippling in the violet light. She glances back at me. Her pale face is tight with worry but she attempts a small grin. *I'm glad I had a blood boost, though. He's fast!*

Just like his mama sire. I smirk at her. *He's got your power as well as mine. Luckily, Hester didn't give him her blood. Otherwise, he'd have hers too.*

I glance sideways at Hester running silently next to me. She doesn't utilise her shape-shifting power in the present day. She said it came in useful during the Tudor period, but there's not really any cause for her to use it now. I'm kind of glad she doesn't as I'm insanely jealous she can, and she knows it. I'd sacrifice my favourite pair of stilettos for that ability.

Hester raises an eyebrow at me. *That would be interesting. Maybe I should give him some to see if it would take.*

Don't you dare, bitch!

Hester and Floss snicker.

Irritated, I block both of them for the moment and focus on my conversation with Tim instead, which is puzzling me. He was slicing up a hunk of bloody steak in the kitchen wearing a blue-and-white striped apron when I came into the kitchen.

'We're popping out for a bit,' I said, leaning against the counter. 'Damian wants to ... er ... go for a run. And we'll keep him company.'

Tim paused with his knife in the air. 'A run at this time of night? It's dark and raining.'

'We can all see quite well, and rain doesn't bother us.'

Tim placed the knife down on the chopping board and turned to face me, looking suspicious. 'Did something happen upstairs just now? I heard noises. I didn't want to interfere.'

I chewed my lip, not sure how to put it. Probably best to

come straight out with it. 'There was an ... accident. We had to turn Damian.'

Tim's mouth slackened in shock. '*What?*'

I shrugged. 'Yeah, he's now a vampire. Kind of bad timing. But it was always going to happen since he's involved with Floss. He's got a target on his back, thanks to Alexander.'

Tim looked confused. 'Who's Alexander?'

'Floss's sire—it's a long story.'

Tim had looked at me and exhaled. 'Then maybe this is a good time to turn me too. We should keep it in the family.' He'd said it half-jokingly.

It wasn't a topic that was up for discussion, as far as I was concerned. One newbie vampire to take care of was enough. 'No, Tim,' I'd stated flatly. 'I'm not turning you.'

His expression had soured like he'd eaten bitter lemon. 'Why not? I love you, Sadie. I don't know what else I can—'

'I have a ... partner,' I said, cutting him off but deciding not to reveal what exactly Elliott was to me. Saying that he was my thrall didn't exactly put me in a good light. 'He's been kidnapped by Alexander. We're trying to track him down.'

'Oh,' Tim said. He'd raked a hand through his hair and digested this piece of information. 'But if it doesn't work out with him, maybe you could consider—'

'I'm getting him back!' I'd hissed and left abruptly.

Seriously? Like I'm going to give up on Elliott and choose Tim instead? That's not happening. I can't understand why he's so determined for me to turn him. I'm finding it hard to believe that he has strong feelings for me, though he says he does. We haven't seen each other for forty years!

I suppose I could have poked around in his mind to glean his thoughts, but I was too pissed off to do it then and there. I will when we get back to the house, though. His attitude is bugging me.

Floss gives a distressed cry up ahead.

Me: *What's happened?*

Floss: *Damian's gone off-piste!*

There's the sound of crashing branches on the left.

Me: *Shit! He's making a hell of a racket!*

Floss (mournfully): *I know.*

Hester: *We'll have to follow him. Try to contain him somehow.*

'Babe! Babe, come back!' Floss starts pushing through the undergrowth, and there's nothing for it but to plunge in after her. I hate the feel of sharp twigs scratching my arms and legs, but they're tiny cuts that heal instantly. Luckily, it doesn't go on for too long. Hester and I emerge into a clearing to discover Floss has managed to grab Damian's arms and is keeping a firm hold on him. Thank the Lord!

A branch snaps in the distance, and Damian's head whips up. He sniffs the air in a concentrated sweep.

'What's he smelling?' Hester whispers to me.

'I don't know. A wild boar perhaps?' I reply, unable to detect anything either.

Damian hears me and growls, 'Let's chase it!' It's the first sentence he's spoken since he was turned, and I'm a bit shocked at how husky his voice sounds.

Floss giggles as if she likes it, and her arousal permeates the air. I assume he talks like that to her in bed. Jekyll and Hyde indeed!

Before I can make a snarky comment, Damian's off again, tearing through the trees. I sigh. This is going to be a long night.

***

We give chase, leaping over fallen logs, dodging trunks, and ducking under branches. We're going deeper and deeper into the forest, which concerns me. I thought this would be a quick jog. Now it feels more like a Tough Mudder event.

Me: *Where the hell is he going? I would've put on trainers if I knew we were going forest bashing.*

Hester (gasping): *Don't tell me you're wearing stilettos!*

Me (scoffing): *Please! I'm in Converse, but not the ones designed for running.*

Floss: *Guys, this isn't good.*

Me: *Duh, what have I been saying? My shoes are getting ruined.*

Floss: *No, I mean I'm getting blood bond activation.*

Me: *With Damian?*

Floss: *No, someone else.*

Me: *Oh shit. That means ...*

Floss: *Yup, Alexander territory. Hester, can you shield me?*

Hester: *On it.*

We slow down to a dawdle, nervously peering around as if Alexander is going to pop out from behind a tree trunk and yell 'Surprise!'

Floss: *Don't speak aloud from now on. Use telepathy. In case he's nearby.*

She projects the thought clearly into our minds, and I gape at her.

Floss (happily): *I know, I'm getting better at this. I think my connection to Damian is helping to increase my powers.*

Hester: *Speaking of which, where is our baby vampire? It's gone worryingly silent.*

Floss: *I can sense him. He went this way. Tread carefully and try not to make any loud noises ...*

As soon as she says this, I take a step forward, and my

foot connects with a fallen branch; it snaps in half with a crack that echoes through the silent forest like a gunshot.

We all freeze in place.

Me: *Ah, sorry about that.*

Floss (sarcastically): *And try not to get us drained.*

***

Hester: *Is it Hadrian's Wall, do you think?*

We peer up at the mighty stone fortification blocking our way. Having eventually reached the edge of the forest, this is now the current obstacle to deal with. There still hasn't been any sign of Damian, though Floss insists he's around.

Me: *Don't be silly. We haven't crossed into England! And this is much too high to be Hadrian's Wall.*

Hester: *Great, just checking.*

Floss: *It has turrets and window slits. I think it's a castle.*

Me: *Alexander's castle?*

Floss: *Possibly, though I can't feel him as strongly anymore.*

Me (excitedly): *If it is, Elliott could be inside! We have to get in.*

Hester (cautiously): *Let's not get our hopes up. It could be an Airbnb rental, and we don't want to give the guests a nasty surprise.*

Floss: *Besides, we can't enter unless we're invited.*

Me: *I really hate that rule.*

Hester: *Do you want me to do a little reconnaissance?*

She makes a clawing motion with one of her hands, and I narrow my eyes.

Me: *This isn't the time to show off.*

Hester: *Who said anything about showing off? Floss shouldn't get any closer in case it's Alexander's lair. So it makes sense that I check it out, and my alternate shape is perfect for that.*

Wordlessly, I nod and link arms with Floss. We step back to give her space. Hester crouches down, folds her arms around her body, and mutters what sounds like a spell.

A millisecond later, I blink; and there's a black cat sitting there, staring at us with slanted green eyes. It saunters over to me and butts its head against my leg.

Hester: *Stroke my fur. You know you want to.*

Me: *Oh, sod off.*

Hester: *Charming!*

The cat gives a soft hiss, then bounds over to the castle and trots off following the perimeter round to the right until it disappears.

Floss: *So cool. I wish I could do that.*

Me (jealously): *Yeah, me too.*

Floss: *Do you think Damian's OK? You don't think he*

got inside the castle somehow?

Me: *I'm not sure how he could.*

We wait for Hester to return.

An owl hoots.

Leaf water drips down my neck.

I get cramp in my foot.

A hand taps me on the shoulder, and I almost jump out of my skin. I spin with my fists clenched. But it's Hester, back in her usual form, an amused grin on her face. I drop my fists.

Me: *Well?*

Hester: *So there's good news and bad news.*

CHAPTER 30

Elliott | Highlands, present day

Lucy bares her bloodied fangs at me, and I take a quick step back. Rejecting a woman when she's a newly turned vampire is a stupid thing to do. But I'm a vampire too, so she should be equally scared of me! I hiss and show off my fangs, and we circle each other warily.

'This is dumb,' I remark when we've shuffled around half a dozen times. 'We need to work together. You've got your cat to think about, and I need to get back to Edinburgh.'

Lucy's shoulders relax. 'I didn't really want to kill you anyway. It's just instinctive, you know? I guess I'm going to have to work on that.'

'Yep, it's our bloodlust,' I agree. 'I've been a thrall for ages, so I know how it works. My ... girlfriend ... Sadie, she's pretty good at keeping hers at bay. With my help, of course. But she said it took her decades to control it.'

'Oh?' says Lucy, sounding interested. We fall into step and start walking along a forest trail, which I'm hoping leads to civilisation.

'Yes, and even then, she had lapses where she went on a feeding frenzy.'

'When was she turned?' Lucy asks, holding a branch back so I can pass through.

'Thanks. Um, 1758. In London.'

Lucy whistles. 'So she's ancient then.'

I smile to myself. If Sadie were here, she'd be growling at that remark. To Lucy, I say, 'I suppose so, but she doesn't look it. She stopped ageing at 21.'

'Is she really pretty?'

I nod. 'Beautiful. She's got these amazing blue eyes that pierce your soul. And she's really funny. She says whatever's on her mind. It makes me laugh so much. And she's so strong and fierce and ... bossy. But in a good way.'

My heart stopped beating about half an hour ago, but it must still have muscle memory as it constricts painfully thinking about Sadie and how much I miss her. She must be looking for me, surely? I can't believe she'd sit back and let Alexander take me. Not after forty years of us being ... whatever it is we are to each other.

But what will she do now that I'm a vampire, though? What if she doesn't want me?

'Why wouldn't your girlfriend want you? What do you mean?' asks Lucy curiously, and I realise she's surreptitiously read my thoughts. Shit.

'Nothing,' I say hurriedly, not wanting to be emotionally vulnerable around her. I trust her somewhat, but not entirely. I try to read Lucy's thoughts too but pick up on exactly ... zero. Whatever mental power she has doesn't extend to me. Don't tell me I'm one of those vampires with no special powers at all! That would be a bummer.

Sadie told me all about how she and Floss visited Alexander's son, Charlie, in London in 1921. She said that not only was he a poor excuse for a vampire, but that he'd started ageing as well. She sounded so scathing of him. I felt a bit sorry for the dude. It makes me worried that I'm going to be like him—a pathetic vampire. Sadie will kick me in the shins with her stilettos, and I'll probably let her.

I'm tramping along behind Lucy, attempting to keep my self-deprecating thoughts from her, when she stops in her tracks, head tilted. Listening.

'What is it? Alexander?' Don't say he's been following us all along!'

'Shhhh, can you hear that?'

I strain to hear and pick up on a faint squelching noise coming from the depths of the forest on the right of us. Gosh, Lucy's got great hearing too. Lucky cow. But my supersensitive nose twitches as the distinct scent of blood reaches it. My mouth starts watering. I drift towards the smell, like a cartoon character transported on a food aroma.

'Elliott, wait. It could be dangerous.'

'I don't care.' Suddenly, my appetite is too ferocious to tamp down, and I understand exactly what Sadie has been trying to deal with all these years.

Lucy shakes my arm, rousing me, and I blink at her. 'I know, it smells great. I get it. But let's go over there slowly and quietly,' she says, placing a finger to her lips. 'So we don't startle whatever it is.'

I nod. 'Makes sense.'

We tiptoe through the undergrowth, being careful not to rustle trees or step on branches. Difficult to do when you're five foot eleven with size 10 feet.

The squelching sound gets louder. Lucy tugs me behind a fallen log with moss growing out of it. 'Look, straight ahead,' she whispers urgently in my ear.

At first, I can't see anything. My eyesight doesn't seem as good as hers either. (Is that because I wore glasses as a human? I would've thought turning into a vampire would have given me 20/20 vision. Obviously not!) Then the longer I peer, my night vision slowly adjusts, and I see a snuffling shape bent over a larger darker form on the ground.

'What is it?' I whisper back.

'It looks like a man.'

'What's he doing?'

Lucy makes a sharp shrugging motion, and her shoulder pushes against mine. As I'm teetering in a crouch, I overbalance and clutch at the log. But it too is teetering, and it topples forward to the sound of splintering wood.

The figure stops snuffling and snaps its head up, looking straight at us. Blood drips from its fangs. Lucy gasps in terror, but I know who it is.

'*Damian?*'

He grins and leaves off from whatever he's been doing; and in a flash, I'm lying on mulch, being enveloped in a bone-crushing hug. I shake with relief at being one step closer to Sadie. I *knew* it. I knew she'd come after me!

There's a hiss, and I remember Lucy. I extract myself from Damian's arms, and we scramble to our feet, brushing off dirt and leaves.

'Lucy, this is my mate Damian,' I tell her with a smile. 'He's a dentist but now seems to be a *fucking vampire?*' I thump him on the shoulder delightedly.

'Yeah,' says Damian, looking a bit embarrassed at my announcement. He wipes his mouth with his hand. 'I am.'

'So Floss decided to turn you!'

'Not quite, but she was involved.' He averts his vivid green eyes from mine.

Huh, maybe Floss chickened out and asked Hester to do

it?

But Damian's attention turns to Lucy before I can find out more about his transition. 'Nice to meet you.'

'Likewise,' she says.

'I assume you both escaped from Alexander's clutches? We've been searching for you, Elliott. Sadie is out for blood. If Alexander's around, he'd better watch out.'

My chest swells with pride. 'That's my girl.'

'Yeah, she wants her thrall back,' confirms Damian.

My chest deflates a little. 'Oh. Well, I'm not a thrall anymore.'

I lift my upper lip and show Damian my fangs. He blinks and peers at them. 'Nice pair, mate,' he says. 'Did Alexander turn you?'

'Uh, no. Lucy did.'

Damian snickers, covering his mouth with a dirt-smeared hand. 'Oh man, Sadie's gonna be pissed about that.'

'It was the only way to get out,' I say defensively. 'I'm grateful to her. He had me chained up in his dungeon and was taking my blood for some nefarious experiment. Apparently, he's got a retinue of female thralls doing his bidding. Isn't that right, Lucy?'

She nods, her hand resting on her dress pocket protectively.

Damian cracks his knuckles. 'We'll need to deal with him

then.'

He doesn't seem afraid to take Alexander down. In fact, he's so completely different from terrified human Damian that it's hard to believe it's the same person. He's almost got an air of Sadie's brashness about him.

Speaking of which, I look around expectantly. 'Is Sadie not with you?'

'She's with Floss and Hester. They're around here somewhere. We got separated. They'll find us. Let's feed in the meantime and keep our strength up.'

'Feed on what exactly?' asks Lucy.

Damian's unnatural eyes gleam in the indigo light, which matches the purple streaks in his hair. 'I caught some dinner.'

CHAPTER 31

Sadie | London, 1758

Darkness greets my eyes as I wake. For a moment, I think I've gone blind, then realise there's something soft covering them. Tearing at a silken strip, I sit up to find I'm naked, alone, and lying on a bed that isn't mine. If I'm not at the brothel, then where in God's good name am I? This room, with its dark-green wallpaper and walnut furniture, is wholly unfamiliar.

Crawling to the edge of the wide bed, I'm about to step down when I glimpse a pair of large bare feet poking out from under it. I lean over further to find that the feet are connected to muscular pale calves, neither of which is moving. Darius seems to be under the bed, and I hope he's sleeping.

Trepidation rolls through me. *Sadie, what did you do?*

I rack my brain, but I can't remember anything after Anya told me I was going to be her supper, which I'm sure she was teasing me about. But where is she now?

Her tower of silver coin is stacked on the sideboard next to the bed. So the sequence of events seems clear: Anya ate her bread and cheese, watched Darius and me fuck, and then we all drank ourselves into oblivion ...?

No, that doesn't seem right. It's no good. I can't remember. But there's no point sticking around until Darius wakes up. *He'll just have to sleep it off but I don't envy him his raging hangover.*

I, on the other hand, have no hangover and feel absolutely chipper. Better than chipper, I feel positively radiant. I stand and stretch, catching sight of myself in the full-length oval mirror on the back of the door. My skin is glowing, my golden hair lustrous, and my burnt fingers are healed! I also seem ... taller. But as I get off the bed and walk closer to the mirror, the image wavers and goes transparent. I rub my eyes. But ghostly Sadie is still there. How peculiar. It must be a trick of the light.

Tiptoeing across the floor so as not to wake Darius, I find my stays and yellow dress behind a changing screen, along with a bowl of water and soap. Might as well have a wash while I'm here. When I dip the washcloth into the water after running soap over my body, it turns a murky reddish brown. I suppose it's from some wine I spilled on myself. I'm not normally a big drinker, but if Darius was plying me with glass after glass, then it may have turned into a drinking frenzy. I smile to myself. Sadie Smith is not a girl to turn down free wine! Fortunately, I seem to have handled the excess admirably.

Shrugging into my stays, I give them a cursory tug to contain my bosom and slip my dress over my head. My hair I leave mostly loose, apart from a few pins I stick randomly in it. I can't seem to bring myself to care about looking respectable for the walk of shame back to the brothel. Everyone in the vicinity knows I'm a prostitute, so why try and make out I'm a lady?

I stuff my feet into my shoes, which I also find neatly placed side by side. And there's my velvet drawstring purse. After I swipe in the coin from the sideboard, it's difficult to close it. Last night's takings were the most I've ever earned. Good on me! With this haul, I'm going to buy myself a new dress, some rouge, *and* a pair of silk stockings.

Thinking I might buy some jewellery as well, I pause by the bed, staring at Darius's feet. It's a bit strange that he's lying *under* the bed. I know I should check to see if he's all right, but I feel fearful about that for some reason.

Letting myself out of his house, I squint in the glare of the morning light and can barely see as I stumble down the front path. Strange, I must have a hangover after all, even though I felt perfectly fine inside. Sticking to the narrow alleyways, where it's darker and easier on my eyes, I weave through the London streets like a rat in a maze, operating purely on instinct. If a street 'feels' right, I'll go that way. Somehow, I end up at the back entrance to the brothel without incident. A feat that astonishes me somewhat as I don't particularly have a good sense of direction. Mother Swift never sends me out for her gin rations as I always get lost.

No matter. I'm here now. But thirsty. So thirsty.

I haul myself up the secret stairway, my legs barely able to function and my mouth on fire. *I. Must. Drink. Now.* Several girls are milling around, chatting, when I burst out of the doorway and flop against the hallway banister. They crowd around me, exclaiming in surprise, and help me to my room, burning my ears with a million questions.

'We thought you'd run away.'

'What happened to you?'

'Are you hurt?'

I'm pleased at their concern but unable to give them any sensible answers. All I can rasp is 'Drink' and 'Thirsty'. One of them runs off to her room for a jug of water, and I sit on my bed and gulp it greedily while they all stand around and watch.

But I'm still as thirsty as ever when I finish, and now I feel nauseous. With a heaving retch, I vomit the water violently back into the jug. The girls all take a step back.

'She's ill,' whispers one.

'She's caught something,' says another.

I feel so odd. So cold. I need to sleep.

The jug is taken from my hands, my shoes removed, and I curl under the covers with a shivery sigh as the door closes.

Blessedly alone at last.

A cool hand brushes my forehead, and something pours down my throat in a smooth sweet river. But it's not real. It feels like I'm remembering something from a dream.

Sleep now, little one. And you will drink again.

***

A sharp rap on my door rouses me, and my eyes snap open to find a purple glow decorating my room.

'Sadie, are you decent?'

I mumble something in the affirmative and sit up as the door opens. Mother Swift enters with a candle.

'Are you well or poorly?' she asks, peering at me. I note she keeps her distance.

I flex my fingers and roll my shoulders.

'I feel ... quite well,' I tell her. And it's the truth, apart from still being terribly thirsty.

Mother Swift breathes a sigh of relief, her large bosom swelling in her red satin dress. Her strong perfume wafts to my nose, making me flinch. Pooh! She's not usually so heavy-handed with it!

'Thank goodness! I thought you may have caught the pox,' she says. 'But it must have been one of those quick passing illnesses. That's why I let you sleep so late. I know it was a difficult night, after the raid, for all you girls ...'

I nod. 'Thank you, I appreciate it.'

'But if you're feeling chipper again, there's a gentleman downstairs.'

'Oh?' I massage my lower back, easing out the sleep kinks.

'Yes, he's not one of your regulars. But he asked for you by name and said he saw you last night. You must've made quite an impression on him.'

She winks at me, and my upper gums throb. I run my tongue over my teeth. They feel a bit too big for my mouth.

Mother Swift is looking at me. 'So should I send him up? He said he'd pay double.'

I remember the gentleman. The handsome one with the lengthy rod. My cunny starts twitching.

I lick my lips. All of a sudden, I can't wait to have him pounding inside me. Or maybe he can go on the bottom this time and lie there while I fuck him and ... bite him. Yes, that seems like an excellent idea.

Slowly, I tilt my neck one way, then the other—the bones

cracking.

'Yes, I'm ready to work,' I tell Mother Swift, fumbling eagerly with the buttons on my dress.

Mother Swift gives a pleased chuckle, no doubt thinking of the nice lot of coin coming her way since she takes a percentage of my earnings. 'That's my girl! Back in the saddle. It's always the best way. I'll tell him to come up now.'

She bustles off, and I lie back naked on the bed, licking my lips and smiling to myself.

Oh yes, Sadie Smith is going to give her well-paying customer the best rogering of his life.

Chapter 32

Sadie | Highlands, present day

Please, please don't let the bad news be that Hester saw Elliott's dead body when she was doing her cat reconnaissance.

Me (warily): *What's the good news?*

Hester: *Elliott was definitely in the castle.*

Me: *How do you know?*

Hester: *I found a barred window that opened onto a dungeon cell. I detected his scent.*

Me: *That ties in with what I saw under hypnosis.*

Floss: *What's the bad news?*

I brace myself.

Hester: *He's not there anymore.*

Me (confused): *Isn't that good news?*

Hester: *There was blood on the ground.*

Me: *Oh, not so good. I thought he was being attacked by someone. It's why I bit Damian by mistake.*

Hester: *I don't think we should hang around if Floss is*

detecting Alexander. And we can't get into the castle to find out anything further. We have to assume Elliott's still alive somewhere in there.

Floss: *Let's go and find Damian in the meanwhile and have a think about what to do next.*

It's as good a plan as any, and I can't come up with a reason why we should stay. Yet I'm reluctant to leave the castle if Elliott's in there—what if he's hurt?

There's nothing for it but to follow Floss as she leads the way back into the forest. We pick up the trail again, keeping our eyes open. Not too far along, the sounds of growling and slurping drift to our ears.

Hester: *Alexander?*

Floss shakes her head. *No, my wayward boyfriend.*

We inch forward. Rounding a clump of trees, we stand at the top of a dirt ridge and peer down. In the clearing below us are three people gorging on a large wild boar. Damian's purple-streaked hair is a giveaway. The thin woman opposite is a stranger. But when the person next to her shifts position, I catch a glimpse of a familiar, albeit blood-smeared, face. His shiny white fangs are clearly visible, and they plunge afresh into the boar's neck. Oh no no no no! Elliott's a vampire. This wasn't meant to happen. I'm the only one who should make that decision!

My body trembles uncontrollably. Somehow, I find my voice.

'Elliott John Blythe!' I call out in a deadly tone. 'What the *fuck* are you doing?'

Elliott looks around, then up to the ridge. His gaze lands on me standing there with my hands on my hips. A grin spreads across his face as we descend into the clearing. His bright blue eyes, startling against the vermillion blood on his cheeks, are locked on me. My face remains unsmiling.

'Hey, babe,' says Damian to Floss.

'Um, hey,' she replies, sounding equally shocked at finding her boyfriend feeding from a hairy animal.

Elliott frowns at me. 'Aren't you going to say hello?'

'Hello. Glad you're alive or, should I say, *unalive*,' I say dryly.

The skinny girl crouched next to him on her haunches chuckles. She flicks a patch of bloodied fur off her fingers and stares at me. 'Sadie, right? Elliott said you were funny.'

I bristle at that. 'Who are you?'

'I'm Lucy, Elliott's sire.'

Elliott quickly elbows her in the ribs, but it's too late. Jealousy floods my system. Oh, so *she* turned him. No doubt they've consummated that little arrangement. I know what it's like when you first get turned: you're high on bloodlust until it's satiated.

'How cosy,' I say in as neutral a tone as I can muster. I'm not going to let them see how devastated I am. To find

Elliott, *my* Elliott, only to lose him to this bitch. I can feel the girl's fingers pressing against my brain, trying to push through my mental wall. *How dare she!* I block her instantly. I need to get out of here.

'I'm going back to the house to check on Tim,' I say curtly, turning on my heel and walking off. I make sure to keep my head up and shoulders squared. Damn the lot of them!

'Not Tim, her ex-boyfriend?' I hear Elliott querying behind me. Floss mutters a reply, but I'm walking so fast I'm out of range before I can hear what she says to him.

Rage and despair mix with relief that he's alive. But smack bang in the middle of that is the image of Elliott and Lucy feeding happily next to each other. It's imprinted on my brain. And the fact that *she's* his sire, not me! He'll always have a blood bond with her now, goddamn it. She's obviously the one who helped him escape. Who knows what else that horny little bitch has been doing with him in the castle—

'Sadie, wait up!'

Footsteps slap on wet leaves behind me, but I don't bother looking round. He can go to hell for all I care!

'Just slow down, would you?' Elliott grasps my shoulder, and I round on him with a snarl.

'Don't touch me! Don't ever touch me again!' My words

lash out like a whip, and Elliott recoils. But I don't even know what I'm saying right now. I want to hurt him like he's hurt me.

'I know what it looks like, but it's not what you think,' he says carefully.

I fold my arms and lean against a tree. 'Really? I'm thinking it's *exactly* how it fucking looks. So explain to me how you're a vampire right now.'

Elliott wipes his face with the bottom of his T-shirt, giving me a flash of toned abs. Desire coils tightly in me, and I look away. This is not the time to get turned on by him, even though I'm craving his touch something chronic. But I'm not going to admit that!

'Lucy saved my life. I would've died if she hadn't turned me. Alexander was drawing so much blood ... and I still don't know why. He's swanning around in that castle like bloody Hugh Hefner. You should see him—dressing gown, cravat, the whole works. He looks like a right numpty.'

My lips twist at that, but I flatten my mouth instantly.

'So what happened after Lucy turned you? Did you and she ...?'

'No!' Elliott takes a step closer to me, and I let him (for now). 'All I could think about was getting back to you.'

I humph at that. 'Sure.'

'It's the truth. She was trying it on with me, but I pushed

her away. She nearly bit me again.'

I close my eyes briefly, imagining how good it would feel to rip her throat out myself.

'Isn't it better to have me like this than dead?' he asks, sounding closer.

I open my eyes to find he's right in front of me, looking down with a grin. I can feel myself melting under the flame of his gorgeous smile; it gets me every time. 'Of course. But ... *she's* your sire, not me, Elliott!' I wail.

His arms go around me, and I sag against his blood-splotched chest, whimpering. He caresses my back and cups a large hand protectively around the back of my neck.

'I know, sweetheart. It sucks big time. I wanted you to turn me for so long. But I don't regret it, not if it means I get to be with you forever.'

'I was so scared when Alexander took you. I thought that was it. Then I got so mad. I wanted to kill him!' I growl against his chest.

Elliott chuckles. 'That's my girl. I knew you would.' He kisses the top of my head, and some of my pain and anger dissipate. But I still want to kill Alexander for putting me through hell.

'How did you find me?' he asks.

'Hypnosis. Damian put me under, and I managed to connect with you. It was going well until I thought you were being attacked, and I kind of ... bit him.'

Elliott tenses. 'What?'

I lick my lips. 'Yeah.'

He pulls back and looks down at me with a serious expression. 'So why are you giving *me* shit when *you* turned Damian?'

I give a nervous chuckle. 'Er, well, technically, Floss gave him her blood to transition him. But mine was still in his system. Now he seems to have a combination of both our powers: telepathy and speed.'

Elliott huffs. 'Lucky him! All I've got is a supersensitive nose.'

I giggle at that. 'Really? Surely, you've got something else?'

He shrugs. 'Not so far.'

I rub his arm. 'It doesn't matter to me.'

'You're not going to ditch me if I turn out to be a pathetic vampire like Charlie?'

Frowning, I shake my head. 'No, of course not. I want you just the way you are.' My chest tightens, and my bottom lip quivers, feeling vulnerable.

'I want you too.' Elliott tilts my head back and runs his lips down my throat. 'And a sensitive nose isn't the worst thing in the world. You smell delicious to me right now.'

He presses me back against the tree, his hard length

nudging the apex of my thighs. I'm usually the one in control of things, but part of me is liking this new take-charge Elliott.

'I want you to take my vampire virginity,' he whispers in my ear.

I smile at that and look around at the forest and its glowing purple trees. 'Here?'

He nods. 'Right here. Right now.'

CHAPTER 33

Elliott | Edinburgh, 1983

Perhaps it's the noise or the sensation. Whichever it is, it jerks me from my dreamless slumber in the dead of night.

My eyes slit open to find Sadie crouched over my lower half. She's doing something to one of my thighs. I can feel the rhythmic suction of her lips on my flesh, hear quiet slurping …

What the hell? She's drinking my blood!

I attempt to haul myself into a sitting position. But I'm so weak I can barely lift my head off the pillow. I curl my right hand into a fist, thinking that with one good blow, I can knock her off me. Yet I falter as I don't want to hurt her. And what she's doing isn't really that bad, is it? She told me she was a vampire. She *proved* it to me, so she was telling the truth, and she needs to feed. And somehow, I trust that she won't take more than she needs. All this seems logical, and I lie there obediently until she's had her fill. In some ways, I feel proud, like I'm glad I can be of service to her. Like I've found my true calling.

Sadie lifts her head with a sigh and wipes her mouth with the back of her hand. 'Your blood is so yummy, Elliott,' she murmurs as if to herself. 'I could drink you for hours.' I tense at that, and she chuckles softly. 'But I won't, of course. I need to keep you alive.'

I relax again, and there's a touch on my thigh, like she's rubbing her thumb over the puncture marks she's made. Strangely, it didn't hurt when she was drawing blood. It felt kind of ... nice, even a little *arousing*. As she said, she's had 225 years of practice, so she's an expert at making her victims relax and do her bidding. If I struggled and thrashed around, it would make her job a lot harder.

Not that I'm a *victim*. I'm helping her out willingly, of course!

Glancing down curiously, now that Sadie has moved back from my thigh, I'm shocked to discover that my boxers are around my ankles. I'm naked from the waist down! Not only that, but my cock is standing proudly to attention. I make a small murmur of protest, and Sadie's attention flicks to me.

'Did you say something?'

I open my mouth and attempt to speak, but nothing comes out. She giggles. 'Oops, I forgot I silenced you.

Sorry.'

My voice comes out in a harsh rush. 'Pull up my boxers *now*!'

There's a surprised pause, as if she wasn't expecting me to get shirty. 'OK, OK, keep your hair on. I didn't want to get blood on them as *I'm* the one who's doing your washing.'

My boxers start travelling up my legs of their own accord, then stop when they're midthigh level. 'Although ...' Sadie is staring at my cock with her head tilted. 'It's going to be difficult to get them up over *that*, even with my superior powers.' She sniffs. 'I mean, it's pretty ginormous. You must've been enjoying my feed.'

I glare at her. 'I wasn't,' I lie. 'It was horrible. Why would you think I'd enjoy you drinking my blood? That's ridiculous.'

Sadie trails her cool hand up my leg to rest close to my balls, and my dick twitches involuntarily. 'Oh, I don't know. I've heard that it can feel quite erotic.'

'Who from?' I ask suspiciously.

She shrugs. 'Various men, in a previous life.' She eyes my length and licks her lips, as if she wants to devour it. 'I could help you out. You have a lovely one.'

My cock starts glistening at the tip, like it's keen on the idea of her touching it.

'No thank you,' I say in a strangled tone. But how I'm going to fall asleep with this hard-on is beyond me.

'Are you sure?' Sadie's cold finger traces up the underside of my hot cock, swirls in the pre-cum leaking out, and trails back down again to the base. She does this a few times, and at last, I let out a little moan. I can't help it. It feels so good. And it makes sense: her jerking me off would *help*, and it would be weird if I did it myself with her here. Not that I can lift my hands anyway. My right one is still curled in a fist; it never even made it off the bed.

'OK,' I say breathlessly. 'Just to help me out.'

Sadie smirks. 'I knew you'd come round to my way of thinking eventually.'

She slides a hand around my cock and starts stroking it firmly while her tongue flicks out, licking and tasting the tip, making 'mmm' noises in the back of her throat. My eyelids flutter shut at the sheer pleasure of her touch and that she's enjoying herself too. *I like that. I like that I'm pleasing my girl.*

My eyes shoot open again at that. My girl? Where did that come from? I gaze at Sadie, now suctioning her lips over my cock and wish I could touch her too.

'Can I ... can I do anything ... for you?' I ask hesitantly.

She pauses midsuck, as if thinking, and shrugs. My hands lift free off the bed, and I eagerly push up her short skirt.

I'm faintly shocked to find pale bare buttocks underneath and no knickers. But not entirely surprised. I mean, she is a dominatrix vampire who whips men. She's probably always up for it.

While Sadie sucks on my cock and the heat rises in my belly, I can barely think of anything but making her feel the same way. I drive two fingers into the depths of her pussy, pleased to feel that her slit is soaking wet. Cold, but wet. Did I do that to her? I reach around with my other hand to find her clit and give it a slow rub, causing more moisture to coat my hand. Oh yeah, she's definitely turned on by me. Sadie's lips and tongue are doing exquisite things to my cock, and I can feel myself starting to lose it. Quickly, I piston my two fingers and roll her clit between my forefinger and thumb. *It would be nice to come together!*

Sadie's groans reverberate around my length as she deep-throats my cock. But all I can think is *Hold it together, Elliott, and keep it nice and steady on her slit and clit.*

Electricity zips up and down my spine as Sadie sucks, swirls her tongue, and squeezes my balls. It's so good, too good. I groan loudly as my fingers pick up the pace, fucking her pussy rhythmically.

My cock explodes in her mouth, and a thick pulsating stream of cum coats the back of her throat. There's so much of it, and it seems to go on forever, yet Sadie gulps and guzzles it down thirstily.

My fingers must be doing a good job of their own as she stops mid-gulp and tosses her head back and moans with pleasure, my cum dripping down her chin. Her pussy clenches around my fingers, and her swollen clit pulses. Aha, I made her come too. I'm glad about that. I withdraw my saturated fingers, giving them a lick for good measure. Mmm, she tastes so good; her essence makes my lips and tongue tingle.

Sadie grins, watching me, as she wipes my cum off her chin. 'That was lovely, Elliott.'

I smirk. 'Yeah?' Inside, I'm bursting with pride, like I've fulfilled my main purpose in life or something.

'Yes, we make a good team.'

A *team*? Hmm, that sounds vaguely business-like, not like lovers or partners or, God forbid, girlfriend and boyfriend. Which is what I'm starting to think of us as. I need to temper my expectations. I'm sure after I make her come a few more times and we start having proper sex, she'll think of me like that too. I'm convinced of it.

CHAPTER 34

Sadie | Edinburgh, 1983

During the next week, I compel Elliott several times to make me come while I feed and suck him off. From his moaning and gasping, I can tell he enjoys it as much as I do.

Besides, there's not much else to do while Floss and Hester are out with real estate agents finding us a new flat. Of course, they don't know that I'm now getting fingered and giving the hired help blow jobs. But honestly, how do they expect me to keep my hands off him, for Christ's sake? Elliott is soooo sexy.

And it's not like we're paying him exactly. When we get to the new flat, any shenanigans between us will stop. It will be strictly a business arrangement. I'll make sure of it.

* * *

One afternoon, we're lying together on the bed, and I get in the mood. It's difficult not to when I've compelled him to take his T-shirt off. I give Elliott's hand a mental nudge to stroke my leg, but when I take off my top and bra and pull up my skirt, he gives a groan and rolls on top of me. It's like his lust is taking over, and I hardly have to compel him at all!

I ease down his jeans and boxers until he's naked. He nudges his erect cock at my wet entrance. 'Yes, that's right,' I murmur encouragingly. 'Fuck me, pretty boy.'

Elliott doesn't shy away from that. He eagerly inserts his cock, which feels delightful. Soon, he's moaning and thrusting in and out of my pussy until I'm gasping with pleasure. I come so hard I see stars! Moments later, Elliott jerks, and his warm spurting cum thaws my frozen insides. Mmm, I could get used to this. He really is a delicious thrall and perfect in every way.

After he withdraws silently and we've tidied up, Elliott reaches over to the nightstand, grabs his Walkman, and offers one of the spongy orange earphones to me. We listen to 'Save a Prayer' while he rubs his thumb gently on my arm, and I close my eyes.

'Do you hate me for stealing you from your life?' I ask.

He turns down the volume. 'I did at first, but I feel better now that my Mum isn't worrying about where I am. Thank you for that. I *have* always wanted to try the rural life ...'

Compelling people over the phone is quite easy for me, and I was pleased at the story I came up with to explain where Elliott had disappeared to. He had met a girl (moi) on the Australian leg of the Duran Duran tour and he was now living in The Outback and raising emus. I set his mother's expectations that it usually takes months for correspondence to arrive from there to the UK, so she shouldn't expect a letter from him any time soon—if ever. But that he was safe and well, and to tell all his friends the good news!

'You're very welcome.' I press my temple against his shoulder briefly. I'm glad he's enthralled otherwise he'd be giving me hell about making up bullshit.

We keep listening to Simon singing softly about dreamers taking a chance. Then Elliott asks, 'What happened with you and that guy Tim from upstairs?'

My bare toes curl at the mention of his name. 'He asked me to marry him. In the kitchen of all places, which wasn't very romantic,' I scoff, remembering the coq au vin bubbling away behind Tim's head on the stove as he knelt before me. 'I said no for obvious reasons, so we parted ways.'

'Did you say no coz you're a vampire?'

I nod. 'Yeah ... And well, I like him a lot, but I don't *love* him or anything.'

Elliott exhales slowly, but I can't read his mind, so I

don't know what he's thinking.

'Was he sad?'

'Well, he didn't cry.' I shrug. 'I'm sure he'll get over it. I'm kind of forgettable.'

Elliott lowers his earphone and looks at me. 'What?'

'Nothing.' I clear my throat. 'I was thinking, once we move flats, it might be a good idea for you to have your own place nearby. We can't keep sharing my bed.'

Elliott shifts slightly away from me. 'How would that work since I don't have a job?'

'We'd pay your rent and bills. It would be a business arrangement.'

'What about ...?' He gestures between us.

'A business arrangement with benefits,' I say quickly, deciding that I don't want to cut off my nose to spite my face. Elliott is really good in bed, and I have needs.

He sighs. 'Do I get any choice in the matter?'

'Not really,' I reply, trailing a hand down his smooth chest. 'Not now that you're my thrall. But who knows, I may decide to finish with you after five years. It depends on how well you keep me fed and sexually satisfied.'

'Right. Five years, I can do that. I can be your thrall for five years. And don't worry, fulfilling your desires is my top priority,' he says earnestly.

I know he has to say that because he's enthralled, but it's

still nice to hear it.

'Or ... if you get bored, you could just turn me,' he suggests idly.

I gape at him. 'No!' I say sharply.

'Why not?'

'I'm not turning you. End of discussion.'

Elliott pouts and turns up the volume of the Walkman until Simon's lovely voice is quite painful for my supersensitive hearing. But I put up with it because I don't want to show any weakness. I lie there, fuming.

Turn him? What the fuck? How dare he!

But underneath my rage is fear, the memory of something bad threatening to surface. I push it back down into the murky pond with a shudder.

It's definitely much safer for Elliott if he's a thrall rather than a vampire. That way, I can look after him and protect him, and he won't leave me.

I can't even imagine what he'd be like as a vampire anyway. If he was, what would his power be? And would we be able to talk to each other telepathically?

But there's no point thinking about it. My decision is final. I'm not turning him—not now, not ever!

Chapter 35

Elliott | Highlands, present day

'I thought I'd be able to talk to you telepathically if I was a vampire,' I say, kissing my way along Sadie's jawline and burying my nose in her hair. She smells so good. I nibble on her earlobe, careful not to dislodge her gold ear cuff, and snake an arm around her trim waist. 'But no go.'

She seems her usual self again, thank God. I thought after she'd discovered Lucy had turned me into a vampire and stormed off in a rage, that was it for us. But the way she's leaning into my touch now suggests she must've been worried shitless about me.

'Yeah, me too. I'm just getting static. That sucks balls,' she murmurs, and I chuckle.

'Knowing how much you hate Hester reading your thoughts, I doubt you'd like it if I did.'

'I wouldn't mind if it was you,' she says softly, pulling down my zipper. A fire ignites in my belly as she touches my hard cock through my briefs. I haven't washed in days, but she doesn't seem to care.

'Mmm, bite me if you want,' I say, angling my neck towards her lips as I can see her fangs have extended. I have scratchy stubble (which she hates), but I know she must be craving my blood. My own fangs are extended and itching to sink into her flesh, yet I hold myself back. This is about her.

Sadie strokes my shaft, and I moan, wishing we weren't in a goddamn forest right now. But she's hesitating.

'Go on, take a drink, gorgeous,' I urge. 'I'm OK. I'm at full capacity from the boar.'

'I want to, but ...' Sadie flinches, fear flashing in her eyes. My eyebrows draw together at her reaction. I've never seen her afraid of anything.

'What is it?'

'I just ... I can't,' she gasps. Sadie yanks her hand from my cock, and I mourn the loss of it.

Low voices float on the air, and I take a step back and hastily zip up. Sadie's mouth sets, and her blue eyes frost over when she hears Lucy's high-pitched giggle amongst the others.

I wish I could convey my thoughts to Sadie, about how much I *don't* want Lucy. About how much I want *her*. Uncertainly, I hold her hand as we wait for them to catch up, and she lets me. It's enough for now. However, I sense it's not the others' untimely arrival that freaked her out. It's something else.

***

The sky is rosy streaked as we tramp across a dew-laden field towards a modern-looking wood and stone house. It has a slanted roof covered in solar panels.

Now I'm the one who's freaking out, knowing that I'm about to meet Tim Rhodes, Sadie's ex. The only guy who's ever proposed to her, as far as I'm aware. OK, she turned him down. But still. He took the initiative and asked her, so I do have a grudging respect for him.

Despite the unresolved issue with Alexander, the mood within our little vampiric group was positive on the walk back. The general consensus was that the jaunt into the forest had several great outcomes. These included finding me and Damian getting fed. 'As well as gaining a new vampire friend!' added Floss.

'Thank you,' said Lucy. 'It's really great to meet you all.' She smiled at us but kept well away from Sadie, who was gnashing her teeth next to me.

I've never seen her so territorial. The way she's acting makes me feel confident that she doesn't have unresolved feelings for Tim. That she wants only me. But there's still something going on with her.

We pause outside the front door to adjust our clothes and flick twigs and dead leaves out of each other's hair. Yet Damian and Lucy have dried blood crusted around their mouths, and I'm sure I don't look any better.

'Isn't he going to freak having six vampires turn up on his doorstep when only four left last night? I'd be running for the hills,' I say.

'Tim's cool,' replies Sadie. 'He's got his own agenda.'

I'm not entirely sure what she means by that.

Damian rings the doorbell, and we wait. But there's no sound of footsteps heading our way.

'Perhaps he went out?' suggests Hester.

Or ran for the hills, I think privately.

'His car's still there.' Damian tries the door handle, and it swings open to an ominous silence. 'This should be locked,' he says, sounding worried.

The familiar scents of roses and expensive aftershave flow to my sensitive nostrils. I sniff them warily. Oh no, should I say something?

Floss beats me to it. 'Alexander was here,' she says flatly.

Everyone freezes.

'Oh dear,' whispers Lucy to me. 'Poor Uncle Tim. He's a goner.'

Before I can grab her, Sadie slips around Damian and

races into the house.

'Wait, he might still be—'

But she doesn't listen. *Goddammit!* My legs take off after her like we're joined by an invisible thread. Where she goes, I go. I just wish I had a weapon. My tongue inadvertently touches my fangs—oh right, haha, I do! Alexander is going to feel these sharp puppies in his neck if he lays a hand on my girl.

A quick head poke into an airy lounge of muted brown and stone decor shows me it's empty. But then there's a loud cry from the adjoining room, and I quail. *No you don't, motherfucker!*

I burst through the door into a state-of-the-art kitchen, fangs bared and fists clenched. But there's only Sadie, crouched over a middle-aged man lying on the floor. He's wearing a blue-and-white striped apron; and I assume, with a sinking feeling, that it's Tim.

He doesn't look good: eyes closed, face grey, and two fang marks in his neck weeping bright red blood. Strangely, he's grasping a plastic spatula in one hand, as if he was using it as a weapon.

Sadie looks up, wild-eyed.

'Quick, get me a sharp knife!' she hisses, and I head towards the knife block on the counter. But she changes her mind before I get there, muttering, 'There's no time.' She rips into her wrist and holds it over Tim's lips. 'Drink, please drink,' she moans.

The others quietly enter the kitchen and gather round. There's a hushed silence as we watch Sadie's blood dribble uselessly out of Tim's mouth and form a puddle on the floor beside his head.

Hester bends and places a hand on her shoulder. 'I think he's gone ... We're too late.' It's what we're all thinking. It looks like he's been dead for hours. Alexander must've tracked Floss's scent to the house and decided to have a midnight feast when he discovered Tim alone.

Sadie lets out a choked cry. 'No!' She opens Tim's lips and rubs her blood over his lips and teeth, making sure it drips into his mouth, but it doesn't do anything. She tips her head back and lets out a screech of fury.

Damian is as white as a ghost. He rakes a hand through his purple-streaked hair and it stands on end. 'Fuck, *fuck*! This is all my fault. What am I going to tell Dad?'

Not only that, I think. *But you'll have to explain to your dad why you've now got glowing green eyes and fangs ... not an easy conversation!*

Floss hugs him, muttering that it's not his fault. That it's her scumsucker of a sire's fault, and even more, that it's *her* fault—she should've staked him in 1921.

I lean against the counter and drag my hand over my

face, knowing that Tim's fate would have most certainly been mine if Lucy hadn't turned me last night.

Speaking of which, Lucy is the only one who doesn't seem too concerned. She steps forward, reaches into her pocket, and hands Hester a syringe filled with red fluid. 'It's a long shot, but try this. In his heart. It's potent.'

Hester doesn't hesitate. She rips open Tim's shirt, plunges the needle into his hairy chest, and pumps in the lot à la *Pulp Fiction*.

Sadie comes over to me, and I put my arm around her. We all stare at Tim sprawled on the floor. The only sound in the room is the creak of the window frames as the breeze picks up outside. Sadie's fingers find mine, and she buries her head in my chest. 'I can't look,' she whispers.

For a minute, nothing happens. But then the spatula twitches. Once. Then again. Then Tim's left foot.

'Look, I think something's happening,' I whisper to her.

Sadie turns around and gasps as both of Tim's feet, his legs, his arms, and then his entire body starts twitching. Even his crotch. I cover Sadie's eyes when that starts happening, but she pushes my hand away impatiently. He jerks and writhes around on the floor like an electric eel, bloody froth oozing from his lips.

Astonished, we all stare, not wanting to go near him. Eventually, the juddering stops, and Tim's eyes fly open. He lies there, looking up at the ceiling fan, blinking.

Sadie takes a cautious step forward. 'Tim? Are you—'

Before she can finish, Tim lets out a snarl, pushes up from the floor, and leaps onto the kitchen island. Dropping to a crouch, he rips away the front of his corduroy trousers and palms his erect cock through the gaping hole. Huge fangs extend from his mouth, and venom drips down his chin. He whines and growls and pants as he jerks off frantically in front of us, seemingly unable to control himself.

Oh dear. I cover Sadie's eyes again and Hester's!

'See,' says Lucy proudly, gesturing at the horny slavering beast that was Uncle Tim. 'I *told* you it was potent.'

Chapter 36

Sadie | London, 1758

So this is my life now, for better or worse. I'm a bloodsucker, an abhorrence to nature, a vampire. How it happened, I don't know. Sometime during the night at Darius's house, Anya must've bitten me, but the memory is lost. And it never returns in the days and weeks following when I'm in a bloodlust frenzy.

Things get to the point where I know I have to confess to Mother Swift—I have to tell her that I'm not 'normal' because a gentleman is going to complain about me at some point. I shoo the other girls out of the parlour, so it's just the two of us. From her tense jaw and the clear thoughts I'm picking up (I can read people's minds!), I know what she's assuming.

'I'm not pregnant,' I tell her.

Her elegant features relax under the mask of make-up, and she lets out a breath. 'Thank the Lord. You're my best girl, Sadie. That would be a calamity.'

'You have nothing to worry about there,' I say pleasantly, smoothing my silk dress (a new blue one I've purchased of late). 'But there is something you should know about me.'

'If it's a gin habit, do not trouble yourself. I'm happy to turn a blind eye to the odd tipple. Don't mind if I join you.' Her red-lipsticked mouth stretches into a wide grin.

'It's not a gin habit.'

'Oh. What then?'

I pause, trying to find the right words. 'Something has happened to make me … otherworldly.'

Mother Swift's forehead wrinkles. 'Pardon?'

'Perhaps it's better if I show you.' I pull a sharp kitchen knife out of my pocket, for I have come prepared to demonstrate. I draw the knife across my forearm, and Mother Swift gasps in horror and leaps off the moth-eaten pink velvet couch to halt me.

'Wait! Look!' I command, brandishing the knife to stop her coming any closer.

Her wide kohled eyes lock on to my arm, watching the red gash. Her jaw sags when it slowly but surely heals until there's nothing there. It's as if I never cut myself.

Mother Swift falls back onto the couch, gaping at me in shock. She makes the sign of the cross. 'Are you undead?'

'Yes,' I say solemnly. 'But I feel quite all right about it.'

Mother Swift lets out a small cry of alarm. 'Silly girl, I *told* you not to go off to strange gentlemen's houses! It was the night of the raid, wasn't it? When you came back the next morning feeling poorly?'

I nod, wondering if this was a good idea after all. What if she insists that I leave the brothel? Where would I go?

But I don't need to worry. Her initial fear slides away, and her eyes take on a bright, cunning look.

'This is excellent news, Sadie,' she says with a sly smile.

'It is?'

'Yes, I will tell you why in a minute. But firstly, have you *bitten* any customers?'

'Yeeess,' I say slowly. 'I am sorry, but I was thirsty, and I needed sustenance ... and physical release.'

'How many gentlemen?'

I tilt my head to one side, calculating. 'I would say a dozen in the last month. But they knew nothing when it was happening, and I seemed able to compel them to forget about it afterwards. They paid and went off home happily enough. But they no doubt wondered at their tired cocks and sore necks the next morning.' I smirk, remembering all the lovely fucking and feasting I've been doing.

Mother Swift rubs her own neck distractedly, as if imagining the sharp points of my fangs jabbing her. 'All right. Twelve, not too many. And that's handy you can erase their memories.'

'What are you suggesting?'

'That we say nothing to the other girls for a start. If word gets out that Mother Swift is housing a vampire, then we would be set upon. You will be staked, beheaded, and burned.'

I shudder at that. 'Not my idea of fun. But I've been keeping to myself lately anyway, so no one else knows.'

'Good, good. How much sleep do you need?' she asks.

I shrug. 'Maybe a couple of hours during the day? I have a lot more energy than before, especially after feeding.'

'We should increase your number of customers then. How many could you service during an eighteen-hour period, do you think?'

Closing my eyes, I calculate rapidly without needing to use my fingers. Thanks to vampirism, my mental acuity has increased. 'At four men an hour, around seventy-two men a day.'

Mother Swift's brown eyes glint greedily. Her exact thought is *Sadie is going to make me rich!*

'Excellent,' she says out loud. 'I'll set you up in my quarters at the back of the house where no one can disturb you, dearie. There's a nice big bedroom and an adjoining parlour you can use too. I'll move upstairs into your bedroom.'

'Oh, thank you. That's kind—'

She waves away my thanks. 'It's not kind. It's business.'

'Fine. But I have two requests.'

She inclines her head. 'Name them.'

'That I can feed on two men of my choosing per day and I get five days off once a month.'

Mother Swift's teeth grind as she calculates how much money she'll lose in my absence. *Five days! That's much more than I allow the other girls. Then again, she's going to make me so much money that it's well worth it.*

'It's a deal,' she says, and I nod, smiling to myself.

Mother Swift reaches out a manicured hand to shake on it but then remembers I'm a vampire and withdraws it hastily.

***

A couple of months later, I'm well settled into Mother Swift's new regime. We're even on a first-name basis, so I'm calling her Fanny.

Her worries about my vampiric state being leaked were unfounded as there aren't as many girls working at the brothel now. In fact, there's mostly just me since I'm so efficient. We've expanded into small group servicings since they're popular amongst the elite. This is how it works: A party of half a dozen young toffs are out on the town for a drink. They go visiting pub after pub, getting rowdier and rowdier until they're thrown out. Then one of them has the bright idea of calling at Mother Swift's. They show up sozzled, demanding the best girls. Fanny smiles winsomely, talks them through my various talents, and gets them all hot and bothered. Once they're thinking with their stiff rods, she then charges them triple. Up front. Suffice to say, once they're in my parlour, they're not disappointed. Everyone leaves satisfied, except for two of them, who stay behind until I'm fed. Fucking, feasting, and getting paid well for it—it's an excellent arrangement.

On the downside, I am quite lonely and missing the company of the other girls. Sharing funny stories about our customers and having a laugh at the pub were some of the highlights of working here. Now I spend most of my time being rogered so I can earn my supper.

They should update my description in *Harris's List*: *Sadie Smith, forever 21, silky blonde hair and luscious long legs. You won't get much conversation, but you'll get a fast sweet fuck ... and a sore neck.*

It is slightly concerning that Fanny is putting all her golden eggs in one basket. I'm her ticket to a fancier life, and she's counting on me to get her there. With the extra money she's making comes extra temptation too, of the alcoholic kind.

One slow afternoon, she sends me out on a gin run. She's been knocking back the stuff like no one's business lately because she's upgraded to a better quality of spirit. But it's not for me to judge how she spends her coin.

I memorise the address of the house she's scribbled on a grubby scrap of paper and wend my way through the darkened back alleys, asking directions from whoever I meet. Daylight hurts my eyes, but I discover I can tolerate it for short periods. Enough to bring back a bottle of dodgy gin for my only friend anyway.

Emerging from a particularly dark alleyway, I blink as a familiar row of houses with neatly tended front gardens and a black iron fence materialises. Fear grips my gut as I recognise exactly where I am. According to the directions I've been given, one of these is the gin house. *And that one right there with the dark-green door, number 13, is Darius's house.*

Quickly, I check Fanny's piece of paper: *Number 11, Stukeley Street. Amy Renfrew. Buy the LARGE bottle.*

What are the chances it's right next door! The gin can wait. I have to know. I have to find out.

After carefully opening the gate, I totter up the garden path, peering around nervously. It takes me a while to gather my courage and knock on the door, but when I do, I know it's out of my hands now. Will he be glad to see me?

Or angry?

The door opens revealing a young gentleman with tousled blond hair and his shirt collar undone. This definitely isn't Darius. My stomach gives a cold lurch.

'Yes, can I help you?' he says in a brisk, but not unfriendly tone.

'I-I'm looking for a gentleman who I believe lives here. His name is Darius Vexley.'

The gentleman rakes his gaze over me none too politely. 'Who?'

'Darius Vexley,' I repeat, straightening my spine. 'He is a business acquaintance of mine.'

The gentleman raises an eyebrow and turns his head and calls into the depths, 'Sammy, do we know a Darius Vexley? Young lady at the front door says he lives here.'

After a beat, another gentleman with ginger hair and a matching moustache appears. His deep blue eyes lock on to my bosom and then lift to my eyes.

'Darius Vexley, hmmm. Doesn't ring any bells. But would you like to come in, madam, while we ponder if we do in fact know him?'

Both of them look at me expectantly, and their thoughts aren't too difficult to determine even if I wasn't a vampire: *Pretty thing, I wonder how much she charges. I'd like to see those rosebud lips wrapped round my dick. Should I ask if she can do us a two for one?*

I take a step back. 'My mistake. I must have the wrong house.'

The unnamed blond man suddenly snaps his fingers. 'Sammy, wasn't the previous tenant called Vexley?'

I take a step forward. 'P-previous tenant?'

'Yes,' he continues. 'The landlord said there was some kind of incident, and *Vexley* had done a runner. We never found out more than that, but it must have been urgent as he left all his belongings behind.'

I bite my lip. 'Is he ... Do you think he is quite well? I mean, was there anything to make you think he wasn't well when he left?'

They look at each other and shrug. 'Like what?' asks ginger Sammy.

'Like, uh, blood on the rug or ... or under the bed?'

Their eyes widen at that, and they look at me curiously. Damn, that's got them thinking suspicious thoughts. *Well, well, the little minx, it's always the quiet ones. Did she stick him with her hatpin because he refused to pay? But what happened after that? The constable might want to know about this.*

'Are you sure you don't want to come in, madam? We can have a check under the bed and see if there's anything amiss,' says ginger Sammy, his kindly tone belying what's going on in his head.

I know if I step foot into that house, they're going to try and detain me or force themselves upon me. Either way, it's not going to end well for them. This was a bad idea. My brain is screaming at me, *Leave it alone! Get the hell out of here!*

Without another word to the two men, I turn on my heel and stride down the path, unlock the gate, and walk hastily across the road to the alleyway. From there, I watch as they confer for a minute, then shrug and close the door. But I can't hear their thoughts; the mind reading seems to work only when I'm right next to the person, which is annoying.

I toss up whether or not to collect the gin from number 11, but Amy Renfrew undoubtedly knows who Fanny is and where she lives. So if the two men happen to look out the window and see me going in there, it would be easy enough to track me down afterwards.

Slowly, I make my way back to the brothel with the men's words ringing in my ears. *There was some kind of incident. He left all his belongings behind.*

But is he alive or dead? Did he walk out, or did Anya kill him and get rid of the body? Will I ever know?

With a whimper, I shove Darius and Anya under the potentially bloodied rug and push them down far away from me, where I don't have to ever think about them again. Or wonder if I'm to blame for the whole sorry mess.

Besides, I have more than enough to worry about. Everyone in certain circles knows me and what I do. If there was another raid at the brothel, I'd be the only one getting arrested. And now I have two suspicious witnesses who know I was asking questions about their previous tenant. I'm going to end up in the Clink. I just know it.

I start walking faster, my heels tip-tapping on the grimy cobblestones, as a plan starts taking shape: Me in Paris, dressed in pink taffeta with a fine hat and well-made shoes. A toff on each arm, vying for my affections. Me laughing and flirting coyly. Hmm, the flirting part could be a problem since I can't speak French, but I'm sure it's easy enough to learn. 'Ooh la la' when I clap eyes on their stiff rods should be enough to begin with anyway. And of course, I'll need a different surname if I'm going to start earning my living as a high-class harlot. Smith is much too plain. What about … *Bouffant*? That sounds French and right posh.

Yes, it's all coming together. Pity about Fanny, but she can easily get the girls back once I'm gone. It's time for Sadie Bouffant, sole resident vampire of Mother Swift's elegant establishment, to vamoose across the Channel and look after herself.

Chapter 37

Sadie | Highlands, present day

I stare at Lucy, aghast.

'What the fuck was in that syringe?' I demand, turning away from the spectacle behind me. Damian and Elliott have wrestled Tim down from the island and are dragging him, kicking and snarling, out the door. It's good that he's in the land of the unliving, but I'm sure he's going to be highly embarrassed when he recovers from his extreme bloodlust—or whatever that was.

Lucy licks her lips and stares at the pool of my smeared blood on the black-and-white tiled floor. I don't want her guzzling on that.

I spin her round and bind her arms to her sides with my power. 'Answer me, bitch!'

'Er, I'll clean this up,' says Hester diplomatically. 'While you two ... chat.'

'I'll help you,' says Floss and slinks off to find a mop.

Lucy struggles against my bond, but I'm too strong

despite her being a newbie vampire, something that gives me a lot of satisfaction. I consider squeezing her until her eyeballs pop, but I know Elliott will be angry with me if I do that.

Eventually, she stops wriggling and shrugs.

'Dunno. It's a concoction of Alexander's. It turns humans into vampires instantaneously.'

'No shit, Sherlock,' I grind out. 'So that's his intention? To turn thralls into vampires for his own amusement?'

'I'm not sure. At least that wasn't the initial intention,' she says. 'The early preparation had his own blood and venom, and it didn't do that. That was more of an energy boost, to give him and us thralls increased sexual stamina.'

I shudder. Alexander is such a vile bastard!

'Then when Elliott arrived, Alexander seemed quite excited about drawing and testing his blood,' she continues. 'He locked himself away in the library and seemed to be working on a secret experiment. I sneaked a peek at his notes when I was allowed in to clean. He'd written that Elliott's blood when mixed with his own created a serum that had "superpotent vampire properties". Apparently, he'd tried it on a field mouse he trapped in the kitchen, and it grew tiny vampire teeth and tried to bite his big toe. Then he trapped a female and injected it into her too, and his notes said the two mice had humped for sixteen hours straight. Until they died from sheer exhaustion.'

My mouth falls open. 'Sixteen hours! Oh my god, that stuff is like supercharged vampire Viagra!'

There's an anguished howl from the lounge, and I glance at the kitchen door worriedly. 'So Tim's probably going to die anyway.'

'That was mice. I'm sure your uncle Tim won't die.'

'And you know this because ...?'

Lucy hitches a shoulder. 'I was Alexander's first guinea pig. And his last since I nicked the rest of his syringes.' She lifts her chin defiantly.

I gape. Wow, she's like the world's first test-tube vampire and kind of a heroine for rescuing Elliott *and* nicking the syringes. She's effectively cut off Alexander's access to that stuff in one fell swoop.

'So did you ...?' I look at the kitchen floor, which Hester and Floss are currently mopping up.

'Twitch and rip my clothes off? No. Alexander didn't give me a full syringe. But the little he did give me was enough, and he took full advantage of my highly sexualised state. I wore him out. It's why I sneaked down to the dungeon and bit Elliott. I wanted to keep going.' She giggles, and my grudging respect for her morphs into irritation. I squeeze her throat until her laughter is cut off.

'Hey, I had no control over myself!' she croaks. 'It didn't

seem to affect Elliott the same way, though. Even when he turned, he was fully faithful to you. And I did try to get with him, believe me. He's super hot and a really nice guy. You're lucky. I wish I had a boyfriend like him.'

I humph, feeling bad about my hissy fit in the forest. Elliott was telling the truth. Hearing her, a stranger, call him 'my boyfriend' gives me a wake-up call too. I've never referred to him that way. He's always my 'colleague' or 'friend', or I say that we have a 'business arrangement'. But fuck, who am I kidding? Elliott is the most amazing guy I've ever met, and I enthralled him for forty years because I didn't want him to leave me and find someone else.

Yet he's never complained about it. He's helped us survive all these years, and now that he's a vampire, he's still helping us. I'm starting to think I'm the one who's been enthralled by him rather than the other way round.

There's another loud howl from the lounge, and we all look at one another. 'I suppose we should check on him,' I say, releasing Lucy. But really, there's nothing I want to do less. I didn't want Tim to die, but having him exist in this unpredictable aroused state is making me incredibly nervous.

In the lounge, we discover Tim thrashing around on the polished concrete floor, his shoulders pinned by Elliott, though someone has put a cushion under his head. Damian adjusts the throw blanket from the couch over his lower half. From the way it's tented like a teepee, Tim is obviously still undergoing his severe reaction to the vampire Viagra.

'What should we do?' pants Elliott. He sounds exhausted, and he'll need to sleep soon.

'I can take over,' I tell him. 'Take a break, baby vamp.' He smiles gratefully at me, and I glow a little under his sunshine.

It's the least I can do, love of my life. Of course he doesn't hear me think that, and I make sure no one else does either!

We all perch on the velvet couches while I concentrate on holding Tim in place. Elliott sits next to me, his thigh resting against mine, which is kind of distracting. *Focus, Sadie! Otherwise, Tim is going to do himself an injury.* I purposely avoid staring at his thrusting hips and the enormous bulge under the blanket and focus on his bloodshot eyes and glistening fangs instead. Still, it's difficult to ignore the animalistic grunts and moans he's making. If it wasn't so horrific, it would be hilarious.

'Ideas? Anyone?' I say through gritted teeth.

'There's only one thing that will bring your Uncle Tim relief,' says Lucy slowly. 'And I think we all know what that is.'

'That counts me out,' says Damian, looking a bit

disgusted. 'He is my uncle after all.'

'I'm out,' chimes Elliott. 'Not into boys, sorry.'

'I'm out too,' I say, and I sense Elliott relax beside me.

'I'm in a relationship,' says Floss, taking Damian's hand. 'I want to help, but it wouldn't be right.'

'Aww, babe,' Damian says huskily, kissing her.

'That leaves Hester or Lucy,' I say, ignoring their lip smacking.

Hester screws up her nose.

'I'll do it since it was my idea to inject him with the blood,' says Lucy.

I rub my eyebrow. Horny little bitch! But Hester doesn't seem keen to deal with this particular problem, and I don't blame her.

'Fine,' I say. 'I'll move him to his bedroom, and you can do your ... thing.'

Tim appears to understand what we're discussing as his hips roll, and the tented mast wobbles to and fro, as if attached to a ship on the high seas. Hester glances at me with an amused expression, and I nearly lose it. I shake my head at her. There'll be time enough for jokes later.

'Can someone look after these?' Lucy dips her hand into her pocket and pulls out three more red syringes. 'I don't want him getting hold of it. It might finish him off.' She looks at me. 'Remember the mice ...'

I nod. 'Do you think Alexander has any more?'

'I don't think so. He had these locked away in a wooden box. I think he was a bit afraid of what he'd created himself.'

'What's in it?' asks Elliott curiously.

'I'll tell you later,' I say. 'Can you tuck the blanket around Tim more securely? I'm going to stand him up. But I don't particularly want an eyeful of his ... teepee pee-pee.'

Floss giggles. My lips twist, but I manage to keep a straight face for Tim's sake. Poor guy, he must be going through hell. I had a peek at his mind in the kitchen but backed off immediately—it was like Dante's *Inferno* in there.

As quickly as I can, I get his legs moving up the stairs, with Damian and Elliott hovering in case he or the blanket falls. There's a tense moment on the last stair, when he teeters and nearly tumbles backwards. Floss screams.

But I manage to right him at the last minute, and he ends up in his room, lying spreadeagled on his king-sized bed. By the way Lucy pushes us out of the room, I assume she's eager to get started on Tim's 'healing' process.

Before the door closes, she pokes her head out. 'Oh, by the way, don't be alarmed if you can't get in. I'm going to lock the door on my side, just in case.'

She winks at me. 'See you in sixteen hours.'

Chapter 38

Elliott | Highlands, present day

When we retire to the bedroom she's staying in, Sadie tells me exactly what's in the syringes and what it does. Fucking Alexander, I knew he was up to something despicable when he was drawing my blood. But this? I feel guilty that I've contributed to this 'vampire Viagra' debacle. That my blood can be used to turn people into vampires. My expression must show it.

'It's not your fault, Elliott,' Sadie says quietly. Sitting on the edge of the double bed, she's being careful not to touch my outstretched legs. 'You didn't know you had special blood or what Alexander was up to. Even if you did, how would you have stopped him? You were shackled to a dungeon wall.'

My jaw clenches, trying to reconcile the mix of guilt and anger that rips through me. Like my sense of smell, my emotions have heightened since becoming a vampire. Luckily, my fangs have receded. Otherwise, I'd be in danger of piercing my own lip. 'I could've at least tried to save those other girls. I knew they were upstairs.'

'You were trying to survive,' Sadie states, moving her hand infinitesimally closer to my shin. 'No one blames you. I would've done the same.'

I sigh. That does make me feel a bit better. Resting my head more comfortably against the padded headboard, I eye her, wondering how she's feeling. All the bravado I had in the dungeon, my resolve to tell her exactly how I feel, has fled now that I'm actually sitting in front of her. I'm too chicken to come outright and ask the question 'Is there an us?' in case her answer isn't what I want to hear. I stick with something safer. The villain at hand.

'We need to stop Alexander.' I wave my hand at the three syringes lying innocuously on the nightstand. 'Or else he's going to try and make more of this shit. And if it gets into the wrong hands ...' I shake my head.

'What?'

I'm thinking along the lines of vampire armies raping and pillaging entire cities. But that might be overly dramatic as I play a lot of zombie video games. I don't want to scare her, so I don't say that.

'This serum breeds vampires. Horny, violent vampires, not peace-loving ones like you and your flatmates.'

'Lucy seems OK ...'

I stare at her. 'Lucy got only a small dose. You saw Tim.' In fact, we can hear him right now via the headboard slamming against the far wall.

'But Alexander needs your blood to create more of it,' Sadie says, wincing as a booming cry of ecstasy filters through from next door. It sounds like a victorious rutting stag. 'And ... and you escaped. So the danger is over. We can go home ...'

I shake my head. 'We can't leave those women in the castle. He's abusing them. Lucy is counting on us to get them out.'

Where's my brave Sadie gone? Why is she being so feeble? It's not like her. I try another tack to rouse her fighting spirit.

'Besides, now that Alexander knows my blood is necessary for his experiments, he's going to try and get me back. Do you want a repeat of the other night?'

She shudders and moves closer to me. 'No, that was horrible.'

'It was.' *Getting torn from your arms was my idea of hell.* 'Just the sight of this stuff is giving me nightmares,' I say aloud. 'It's evil.'

I reach over and collect the syringes carefully in my hand. Sadie jerks. 'What are you doing?'

'Flushing it down the toilet.'

'I don't think we should act hastily,' she says, looking at the syringes nestled in my hand.

I glance at her. 'Surely, you're not thinking of trying it?'

'Of course not!'

There's a thump against the wall and a loud masculine moan. I swallow. They're at it again. If they don't settle down soon, I might have to go for a walk.

Strangely enough, the noises emanating through the walls are not turning me on but doing the exact opposite.

'My instincts are telling me to wait before we do anything rash,' Sadie says, taking the syringes out of my hand. 'We'll sleep on it. You need to rest.'

'Maybe lock our door too,' I mutter, kicking off my trainers and flinging the edge of the bedcover throw over me.

Sadie locks the door and lies down next to me on her side, facing away from me. I'm highly aware of our bodies not touching. I close my eyes, but it's really difficult to fall asleep with all the loud sex noises going on next door.

Then a high-pitched giggle and gasps start up from the other side of the room. Sadie's shoulder tenses. Oh no, looks like Damian and Floss are at it too!

'Jesus,' mutters Sadie. 'It's like Mother Swift's all over again.'

'Tell me the story of how you ended up in the brothel

again,' I say to distract her.

She rolls over to face me. 'You've heard it before.'

'Yes, but not for ages.'

Her lips thin. 'There's not too much to tell. I came from rural Kent. I was a farming girl and a beloved only child—'

'Like me,' I interrupt.

She coughs a little and looks guilty. 'Yes. Anyway, when my parents died unexpectedly, a well-meaning uncle brought me to London to live with him in Clerkenwell. I was 16 years old. But after two years of heartily eating his food, he decided that being a harlot was the best thing for me under the circumstances. "It will slim you down and make a woman of you," he said.'

'Wow, eighteenth-century gaslighting,' I remark disparagingly.

'Yeah, totally Well, I cried and begged him not to send me away, especially not to a *brothel*. What would my mother, his sister, have said? He was meant to care for me and find me a husband! But my pleas fell on deaf ears. He knew of Mother Swift's establishment. So a week after my eighteenth birthday, he delivered me like a virgin lamb to her employ. I had nowhere else to go, and she was kind to me. I worked in her brothel until I became a vampire, and then I moved to Paris. That's it.'

'Did you ever see your uncle again?' I ask curiously. 'Did

he ever contact you?'

'No,' she says flatly. 'I never saw my well-meaning uncle again. May his despicable gaslighting soul be rotting in hell as we speak.'

I squeeze her hand gently, and she lets me. Sadie's story always gets me right in the gut. What a long crazy life she's had. It reminds me too that I've known her for only forty years. It's nothing really in the scheme of things. I'm a mere blip on her radar. If we break up, will she even remember who I am a hundred years from now?

***

Eventually, the sex noises stop, and there's quiet throughout the house. But I can't fall asleep. It's weird being like this with Sadie in bed and not holding her. It's like we don't know each other anymore. Or how to be with each other now that I'm a vampire. And why did she react so badly to my suggestion of getting it on in the forest? I thought she'd be into it. Maybe it was in poor taste and not romantic enough? But she hates all that stuff! It's very confusing.

Quite a few hours must pass as when I wake, the room is much darker. The headboard next door is thumping rhythmically against the wall.

I groan. 'Seriously?'

'Yup, they're at it again,' Sadie whispers. She's lying on her back, staring up at the ceiling. No matter how weird it is for me, it must be even weirder for her having to listen to her ex-boyfriend getting it on with Lucy.

'How long has it been going for?'

'Ten minutes. This session should be over soon. I've been timing them. They go in fifteen-minute spurts.'

I chuckle. 'No pun intended.'

She turns her head and smirks at me. 'Oh, very much intended.'

We stare at each other, and the urge to tilt her face to mine and devour her sweet lips is overwhelming. But there's a soft knock at the door, and she slips away to answer it before I can.

It's Hester. 'Sorry to interrupt ...' she says. Through the crack in the door, I can see she's being careful not to look directly into the room. It's a fair assumption that with everyone else getting it on in the house, we would be too, especially with our history. But she's safe on that account.

'You're not,' Sadie confirms. 'Come in. We're just talking.' Is that a note of disappointment I detect or wishful thinking on my part?

Hester settles herself in the armchair by the window.

'Can't sleep either?' I ask. A rapid *thump thump thump* sounds through the wall from the room to the left, accompanied shortly afterwards by a litany of baritone groans on the right.

'No, it's kind of noisy,' says Hester with a grin.

'Did you want me to read a scene with you?' asks Sadie, still standing by the door and seemingly reluctant to rejoin me on the bed with Hester in the room.

'Oooh, yes please.' Hester whips out her phone. 'I'll forward you the script, but only if you want to.'

Sadie laughs. 'It's fine. I'm up for some Shakespeare.'

'Who do you want to be, Olivia or Viola disguised as Cesario?'

'Er, whichever one you're not auditioning for.'

I don't particularly want to be involved, and my head feels like it's full of cotton wool. So I pull on my trainers and stand up.

Sadie's eyes snag on mine, glowing like bright sapphires.

'Where are you going, Mr Blythe?'

'I might go for a walk and clear my head.'

'Hmm.'

I gaze at her, unblinking, waiting for the familiar tug of her grip to keep me here, if that's what she wants. Instead, there's nothing, no tug of the leash. And it's like a light bulb going off in my head: Sadie's spell is broken because I'm now a vampire. I can choose to leave the room if I want to. After forty years of complete enthrallment, even a simple action like this is staggering, and I stumble a little against the side of the bed.

Sadie turns away, looking intently at her phone, but I know she saw the epiphany on my face. She could force me to stay if she really wanted to, pin me to the floor like she did with Tim; it's her main power after all. But she appears reluctant to control me—now that I'm like her. And my main power hasn't been determined. If it's something dangerous, then she's wise to be self-protective.

'You won't go too far? I don't want to have to go running around in the forest again if you get lost. My Converse can't handle it.'

She gives a wobbly smile, and even though I can't hear her thoughts, I somehow know what she's thinking: *He loved me blindly when his will wasn't his own. Does he now? Is he going to bugger off?*

I guess that's what I need to figure out.

'I'll stick close to the house,' I reassure her. It's the least I can offer for now.

'Before you go ...' Sadie rummages in her handbag and takes out my glasses case. 'I brought these with me. I thought you might need them.'

'Thanks.' I put them on with a sigh. Hopefully, my 20/20 vision kicks in soon. Whoever heard of a vampire needing glasses?

CHAPTER 39

Sadie | Highlands, present day

Elliott returns at dusk. I almost collapse with relief when he saunters into the lounge, having been on tenterhooks ever since he left.

Poor Hester had to put up with a very distracted performance from me. I'm sure she'll do fine. She was born to be an actress, even if she doesn't have complete confidence in herself going into the audition. The desire to act alongside Will is making her extra determined to overcome her stage fright, which is admirable.

But I could hardly focus on what she was saying. All I heard were the lines:

> *Lady, you are the cruell'st she alive,*
> *If you will lead these graces to the grave*
> *And leave the world no copy...*

And I immediately sunk into despair about Elliott. If I'd released him from his enthrallment earlier, at least he would have had a somewhat normal life. But he's a 63 year-old in a 23-year-old's body because my venom has kept him young, and now that he's a vampire he can't even have kids! How shit is that? And it's obvious he's regained his sense of identity. It was written all over his face: *She can't tell me what to do. I'm a vampire now.*

I could have, but I didn't dare try to stop him. He needs time and space to reconcile with this new vampiric form. If it turns out that he doesn't want to be with me, then I have to be OK with that. But oh, I'm a selfish bitch, I want him to choose to be with me forever!

Lucy is the catalyst of all my angst, and I could hate her. I want to hate her. But what's the point? It's not her fault. It's mine.

Silently, I hand Elliott a glass of blood, poured from our emergency stock; and he sips it. I know he has blood in his 'revitalising' coffee, but seeing him drinking it straight is so weird. But then everyone is. Even Tim, who's sitting there on the couch, is looking sprightly, if paler than usual. Vampirism will do that to you.

There's a slate board filled with cubes of raw meat on the coffee table. An amuse-bouche to feed seven hungry vampires.

'Dig in,' Tim says, gesturing to it. 'It's still fresh. I put it in the fridge last night before I answered the door and invited in *your friend* Alexander Dryden.'

'No friend of mine,' Lucy murmurs, and he puts a comforting arm around her. She nestles into his chest.

I'm kind of surprised they're a couple. But I suppose a bond has formed from all those hours they spent fucking, and I kind of figured his feelings for me weren't *that* deep. It must've been more desperation for me to turn him than anything else.

Their snuggling makes me miss Elliott. He's not too far away, only over on the other couch, but it feels like a deep dark chasm stretches between us. I studiously drink my blood and try not to look at him.

Tim clears his throat. 'I have a little speech to make. Firstly, I want to apologise for my appalling behaviour in the kitchen this morning. I don't typically jerk off in front of my guests.'

Everyone smiles politely, and there's an awkward silence.

Hester: *For the love of God, someone please make a joke!*

I sigh. 'Tim, I know you wanted to make us pancakes for breakfast, but there are more subtle ways to serve the cream.'

Tim guffaws, and it effectively breaks the tension. Damian cracks up, and Floss and Hester giggle together. Elliott throws me a grin, as if to say 'There she is'. I huff a laugh. It does feel good to let my sense of humour loose. I've had a few good quips up my sleeve today, but I held back due to the seriousness of everything that's been happening. Lucy smiles thinly, as if she doesn't like me being the centre of attention, but she can get over herself.

'Excellent!' says Tim with a cackle. 'Thank you, Sadie.'

I incline my head.

'Secondly', he continues, 'I don't want anyone feeling sorry for me. Sadie already knows this, but I wanted to be turned. I made up my mind as soon as I saw her standing on my front doorstep last night. And I asked her to. If she hadn't done it, I was going to ask someone else.' His eyes slide to Hester, then Floss.

'Really?' says Damian, sounding confused. 'But why?'

Uh-oh. I shift uncomfortably on the couch, the leather sticking to the back of my thighs since I've changed into a miniskirt. But Tim doesn't mention the other part of the conversation about still being in love with me. He says something quite different.

'I had stage 4 terminal cancer.'

'Bullshit!' It pops out of my mouth before I can help it. All eyes swing to me.

'Sorry, but ...' I wave a hand at Tim's muscular physique. 'He looks so healthy.'

'It was a fast-growing brain tumour,' he says quietly.

'But now I'm healed, and I don't have to be afraid of dying alone anymore.'

He tightens his arm around Lucy and kisses the side of her head. 'This whole day has felt like a rebirth. And I'm so grateful to my new girlfriend, Lucy, for turning me. For giving me the gift of immortality.'

Lucy beams at that while Elliott gazes enquiringly at me. I'm not sure what he's getting at.

'I don't care,' I mouth at him, and he flicks his eyebrows and turns away again. Surely, he doesn't think I still have feelings for Tim? Grrr, I feel like jumping on him and pounding his thick skull into the concrete floor. It's you. I just want you!

I drag my attention back to Tim.

'Thirdly, even though my story has a happy ending, that doesn't excuse Alexander Dryden for making me his dinner. I understand from Lucy that he's keeping a bunch of women captive in an Airbnb castle nearby, and that he probably ventured to my house because he detected Floss was here and he wants to kill her. But I find that unbelievable—'

'He does want to kill Floss!' Lucy pipes up before I can get a word in edgeways. God, I don't hate her anymore, but she's *still* annoying. 'He wrote in his journal when he came back from Edinburgh and I sneaked a peek when he was having a thrall orgy with a few of the girls,' she tells us.

'A thrall orgy! Jesus!' Tim looks thoroughly shocked. But sounds slightly turned on again. To my ears anyway.

'Forget the thrall orgy. What did the journal say?' asks Damian impatiently.

'It was along the lines of: "*Maybe not next week, or next month, but rest assured Florence is going to be eliminated for stealing my money, and that human dentist she's hooked up with can die too. It is her fault that I have to resort to such extreme measures to keep the wolf from the door in the modern world.*" Something like that anyway.'

Floss lets out a whimper. 'We're going to be toast!'

'Don't worry, babe. I won't let him hurt you,' Damian mutters looking furious.

'What does he mean by "extreme measures"?' Tim asks.

Lucy shrugs. 'I don't know. The entry ended there.'

'But why does he want to kill Floss? I'm confused …'

'It's like this, Tim. Sadie, Hester, and Floss have been on the run from Alexander for over a century,' explains Damian. 'Floss took half of his money back in 1921. And he's been holding a grudge ever since.'

'Oh. Right.' Tim raises his eyebrows and stares at Floss.

'I know stealing his money wasn't the best decision I've ever made,' says Floss sounding tired. 'But after thirty-three years of being held captive by him, I was desperate.'

'She was,' I agree, 'You should have seen her. She spent a solid month trying to get his safe open.'

'We've done our best to hide and keep out of his way, but I'm well over that now. I just want to be free of him,' says Floss more staunchly.

'Hear hear,' I add, and Hester murmurs her agreement. Not surprising as she's done *a lot* of shielding over the years.

Damian kisses Floss's cheek. 'You don't deserve his wrath, babe. He's a vicious old vampire who's jealous that you're happy.'

She smiles at him gratefully and gives him a smooch on the lips.

'Awww,' simpers Lucy and I roll my eyes.

Tim surveys our group with a grave face. 'Correct me if I'm wrong, but what I'm hearing is that Alexander Dryden is a fucking menace. And that everyone wants him dead.'

We all nod.

'So killing him effectively rescues Lucy's thrall friends, plus removes the target from Floss and Damian's backs.'

We all nod again.

'There are seven of us now,' confirms Hester. 'With a range of powers. Surely, that's enough to take him down? I mean, the odds are in our favour. We'd have to be pretty unlucky if he killed even one of us.'

My blood runs cold as I contemplate Elliott's handsome profile and his golden locks. *Alexander will not be touching a hair on this man's beloved head. He'll have to get through me first.*

'You're all forgetting one thing,' says Floss.

'What's that, babe?' replies Damian fondly.

'We can't get into the castle.'

'Floss has a point,' I say. 'It's not like he's going to invite us in.'

'No,' pipes up Lucy. 'But I can. I was "born" there, so it's my house. Technically, it's Elliott's too.' She smiles at him. '*Since I'm his sire.*'

I take two cubes of meat and masticate them viciously, imagining they're her flesh. So much for not hating her.

Lucy claps excitedly. 'So that's settled. We're going to kill Alexander and rescue my friends!'

'Who's going to kill him exactly?' asks Elliott. 'Any volunteers?'

No one raises their hand.

'We'll all take wooden stakes,' I say after swallowing my mouthful of raw meat. 'Whoever gets to him first will be the lucky one.'

***

We all pile into Damian's dad's car, ready to head to the castle via the road with our motley pile of weapons, including an old rake, a broom broken in two, the handle of a gardening fork, and a pair of wooden knitting needles. It's not ideal, but it's the best we can do.

Tim offered to drive but said he was worried that he might have a bloodlust surge if he smelled a deer and go careening off the road. So he's out. I offered too, but Elliott quickly shot that down in flames. He obviously hasn't recovered from me driving his van in 1983.

Damian is the logical choice. But by the way he guns the engine and takes off down the driveway in a spray of gravel, I'm rethinking the decision to put a newbie vampire behind the wheel.

Sitting on Elliott's lap in the back seat, I dig my nails into his shoulder as we whip around the corner and onto the main road. 'Is he deliberately trying to make us crash?' I whisper in his ear as Damian's foot hits the accelerator. I'm not worried about *my* physical safety particularly, but more about shunting another car off the quiet country road. Stone walls and fence posts whip past the window. 'Perhaps he's trying to prove he's not a namby-pamby driver now that he's invincible.'

'He probably just wants to get it over with,' whispers back Elliott. 'Either that, or he's giving up dentistry and wants to be a Formula 1 driver.'

I snort.

Floss is in front with Hester perched on her lap. She's in cat form since there wasn't room back here. I eavesdrop on their conversation.

Floss: *Ow, stop digging your claws in!*

Hester: *It's not my fault your boyfriend's driving like a bat out of hell. Tell him to slow down.*

Floss: *I don't want to distract him. He's concentrating.*

Hester: *If I end up as roadkill, it's your fault!*

I smile at their bickering and glance over at Lucy and Tim to see if they're listening, but they're snogging madly. I screw up my nose and bury my face in Elliott's neck. He smells a lot fresher since he took a shower and borrowed some of Tim's clothes. It's like history repeating itself.

'What's up?' He peers around. 'Oh.'

'I knew it was a bad idea to bring those two. We'll be searching the castle for Alexander, and they'll be holed up in one of the rooms, pounding away,' I mutter.

Elliott's shoulders shake with laughter. His arms tighten around my waist. 'I missed you,' he says simply.

My lips hover over his neck. I want to bite him so badly, but this isn't the time nor place. We have a job to do.

'I missed you too. I know I've been acting weird …'

He rubs his temple against mine. 'It's OK. It's a weird situation. We can talk about it later—'

Damian slams on the brakes, and we all scream. Luckily,

Elliott has his arms around me. Lucy doesn't fare so well and ends up bottom first in the footwell behind the driver's seat. Tim fishes her out.

'I'm OK,' she says shakily. 'But what's going on?'

'Alexander's coming,' says Damian in a low voice.

'Babe, are you sure?' says Floss worriedly. 'I can't feel anything—oh shit, he's right. I'm getting it now. He's definitely somewhere nearby.'

Wow, Damian has a blood bond with Alexander too, I guess, since Floss is his sire; and he's a newbie, so he's hypersensitive. This could work in our favour.

'Hester, can you shield them both?' I ask.

She meows. I take that as a 'yes'.

'Should we go back or ...?' asks Tim.

Without waiting for anyone to give an opinion on the matter, Damian floors it down the narrow lane to our left and pulls off behind a stone wall and cuts the engine and the lights.

OK ...

I'm unclear as to his thinking. 'Hello, earth to Damian? What are you doing?'

'I'm not sure. But it's safer if we get off the main road.' He sounds a bit freaked out. 'It feels like tugging and burning. Here.' He presses a hand to his stomach.

Floss pats his leg. 'It's OK. It's the blood bond activating, babe. Now you know what I feel. It's great you're trusting your vampiric instincts.'

'I don't like it.'

'I know, but think of it like a safety beacon. It keeps us protected from him.'

Floss comforting Damian and recounting vampire lore are all very well. But it's frustrating sitting here, doing nothing. And as much as I like sitting on Elliott's lap, my neck is getting a crick in it, and Lucy and Tim have gone back to their snog fest.

'I'm getting out to stretch my legs. Let me know if anything changes.'

'I'll come too,' says Elliott.

I shrug. 'Sure, if you want.'

We exit the car, and a black furry form winds around my legs, nearly tripping me up. 'Yes, you can come too, Hester.'

She meows. *Just a little kitty run. I can still shield Floss and Damian.*

The three of us make our way over along the stone wall to the section that faces a stretch of road leading into the forest. I do a scan of the road and the trees ahead, but there's nothing in the frosty silence apart from the hoot of an owl. It's making me nervous.

'Shouldn't you be feeling him too since he's Lucy's sire?' I whisper to Elliott.

'You'd think,' he whispers back. 'But no, I'm a pathetic vampire after all.'

'Don't say that. Your power is just taking a while to come through. It's different for everyone. Isn't that right, Hester? You couldn't shape-shift when you were first turned?'

Green eyes contemplate us from the top of the wall, where she's sitting, licking her paw.

No, that took a year to come through.

'She says—'

'I heard her,' Elliott interrupts. 'It took a year.'

I whack his arm, pleased for him. 'There you go! You can hear Hester. That's amazing! That's a great start.'

'Yeah,' he says, sounding a bit forlorn.

But before I can encourage him further, Hester leaps off the wall in a flurry of fur. *Get down, both of you. Shit shit shit.*

I pull Elliott down into the grass with me.

Me: *What is it? What did you see?*

Hester: *A magical mystery bus of horror!*

Me: *What?*

Elliott: *Don't mind me. Just joining in the conversation.*

I look at him and beam. It's the first telepathic communication we've ever had. *Hell yeah, baby vamp!* I hold up a fist, and Elliott grins and bumps it lightly with his own.

Elliott: *A bus you say, Hester?*

Hester meows and butts at my hip with her head. *Yes, don't look over the wall whatever you do. Stay out of sight. I'll go and warn the others.*

She bounds off.

Me (muttering): *Sorry, Hester, but I need to see this.*

Elliott: *Yeah, me too.*

We inch up the wall until our eyes are level with the top of it. A blast of light hits me right in the retinas, and I wince. Then a black double decker bus is towering over us, strobe lights flashing and dance music playing full bore. As it passes by, I get a quick glimpse of women in their underwear gyrating on the seats and in the aisles. Then another of a blank-faced woman staring out with haunted eyes. She looks right at me; and I duck, but not before I catch a snippet of her thoughts, as if she's projecting them on purpose in a last-ditch attempt for someone, anyone, to save them.

I scoot back down next to Elliott, and we do a hunched-over run back to the car. 'That was Alexander and a party bus of thralls,' I say to the others. 'There must be at least forty of them in there. I caught the thoughts of one of them. She wants to die.'

'Oh no, how awful!' says Floss. 'We have to help them.'

'Did you pick up anything else?' asks Tim.

I bite my lip. 'No, unfortunately.'

'I did,' says Elliott. 'He's taking them to London because his Airbnb rental contract ran out. Get his plan, though: he wants to set up a vampire brothel for his fellow Nosferatu in Covent Garden and charge them a premium. Some of the thralls love the idea of being turned, hence the partying. Others not so much.'

That must've been the one I saw sitting at the window.

'But he needs more of his special serum to do that,' Elliott adds. 'Since I escaped and Lucy stole his syringes, that could be a problem. But he's still got all his notes from the mice, so he's going to try and recreate it synthetically.'

I gape at this. 'Wow, looks like you've got long-range telepathy coming through, which is a great power to have! I'm jelly.'

Elliott takes my hand and squeezes it.

'There's no point storming the castle if Alexander's not there,' he points out. 'And I refuse to drive to London from Scotland, especially with Damian behind the wheel. We may as well go home to Edinburgh and plan our next move. Obviously, we can't let him follow through with his *heinous* plan.'

I raise an eyebrow at that. I mean, I was a prostitute for over one hundred and fifty years, and I turned out OK. But the memory of that girl's stark staring eyes is difficult to forget. 'Vampire whore' probably wasn't at the top of her list of career choices.

Hester clears her throat, and we all look round. Oh, she's back in her normal body now. 'I know it's not as pressing as a horde of vampire prostitutes, but I've kind of also got an important audition in two days' time.'

Ah, yes. That. Back to reality. It looks like our Highland road trip is definitely over. And us not storming the castle is a good thing for the owners of the Airbnb. There would've been a lot of broken furniture, blood splattered on the carpet, and a vampire buried in their back garden.

Chapter 40

Elliott | Edinburgh, present day

After all the build-up of storming the castle with stakes, plus the excitement of finally being rid of Alexander from our lives, we all feel a bit flat. There's no point hanging around at Tim's since we don't need to sleep, and I have to get back and restock our blood supplies. I've got student appointments lined up back-to-back; they're dying to give up their blood for ready cash. And I've got more vampire mouths to feed now, including mine. This is the start of my new life. No longer bound to Sadie's will. Reclaiming my life, however that looks. But to quote U2, another of my favourite bands, will it be with her or without her?

We drop off Lucy and Tim at the house and collect our stuff and then say our goodbyes. They say they'll help us out if we need them to come to London. But there are five of us vampires against one, so as Sadie says, 'Thanks, but we should be cool'. We're all of the same mind. As long as we can get to Alexander quickly enough to stop him turning the thralls, kill him, and effectively free them. Personally, I'm quietly confident that it will be a walk in the park—despite him having superior powers, there is greater strength in numbers.

The atmosphere in the car is contemplative on the way back. No one seems inclined to talk, apart from Floss and Hester (who is in cat form again). They're going over her lines for *Twelfth Night* on Floss's lap. I listen in for the entertainment value. It sounds like a fun play. I hope she gets the part.

I glance over at Sadie, but she's staring out the window, lost in her own thoughts. She seemed fine about Lucy being with Tim. I thought she might have some residual feelings for him, but forty years is a long time to hold a flame. And I'm hoping by the way she hugged him and quickly hopped into the car, that hers has well and truly burnt out.

Me: *You OK?*

Sadie jerks and looks round at me. *Jesus, I'm not used to that!*

Me: *Sorry, I thought I should practise. You know, so I don't have to message you when I'm in the vicinity with a blood delivery.*

Her lips twist ruefully.

Sadie: *You're still doing the donor service then?*

Me: *Of course, why wouldn't I? I need it now too.*

She shifts in the seat. *I thought you might want to ... leave.*

Me: *Leave? Why would I do that?*

Sadie: *Duran Duran is still touring. I'm sure they'd be happy to see you.*

Me (sarcastically): *I can see how that would go. Hey, Simon. Yeah, I've finally recovered from my raging case of genital herpes if you need a roadie. By the way, don't bare your neck in front of me as I'm liable to bite it.*

Sadie grins and licks her lips. *Doesn't sound too bad. Maybe I could come too.*

Me: *No way, I'm not having you get your fangs into Simon Le Bon!*

Sadie (pouting): *Party pooper.*

Me: *Besides, we have to go to London and stake a vampire.*

Sadie: *Oh yeah, back in Covent Garden. Fun times.*

Me (cautiously): *Your old stomping grounds. You might run into Anya if Alexander is setting up a brothel.*

Sadie: *Her! I never want to see that bitch again. She turned me and wiped my mind. And left me to wake up and* find Darius under the bed. It's fucked me up for two centuries, not knowing what really happened. I told myself he was sleeping, but I suspected he was dead. But did she drain him? Or did I do it?

Me: *It was shitty of her to leave you wondering like that. But my money's on Anya draining Darius, not you. From what you've told me previously, it sounds like she preferred women to men. And maybe she memory-wiped you for your own protection? She didn't want your first memory to be traumatic.*

Sadie (sarcastically): *How kind of her.*

Me: *She must've taken a shine to you. Obviously, there's a lot to like.*

Sadie's cerulean eyes glimmer.

Me: *Is that why you never wanted to turn me? You feel bad about Darius?*

Her jaw works. *I've felt bad about him for over two centuries. He said he was the customer I'd never forget, and he was right.*

I take her hand. *What happened to him wasn't your fault, sweetheart. You weren't the one in control of that situation. You can't blame yourself for Anya's actions.*

Sadie chews her lip. *I suppose so. But I think it's why I didn't want to turn you. I felt responsible for him and thought something similar would happen to you if I did. Maybe that got mixed up with thinking you'd leave me.*

Me: *It makes sense but you don't need to worry about that now. I'm a vampire and I still want to be with you, regardless of anything that's happened in the past.*

Sadie sighs and looks down at her lap. *I need some time to process everything ... It's a lot.*

I open my mouth to tell her how I feel out loud, but then close it again. It's not the right time to declare my undying love. Hopefully I've said enough to convey it, but I'm never entirely sure when it comes to Sadie. I may have to go bigger.

***

Two days later, I'm round at the apartment, dropping off a cooler of blood bags. Damian is there as well. He thought going back to work as a vampire might be a challenge, so he's booked unscheduled leave for two weeks to try and control his bloodlust. By the way he salivates at the blood bag when I hand it to him, it could take more than two weeks.

Hester is at her London audition, and Floss keeps checking her phone anxiously. 'Nothing yet. She must've had it by now. She said she'd message me as soon as she heard anything.'

'She won't find out straightaway, surely?' says Sadie from her revolving leather chair.

Apart from greeting me when I came in, she's been ignoring me. It's been like this ever since we got back. No invitation to come over and stay the night either. That strange awkwardness is still there between us, and I'm not sure how to bridge it.

Floss nods. 'They want to make a decision pretty quickly. It's between her and two other girls. Oooh, I hope she gets it. She's perfect for the part, and Will will have to notice her then.'

'Who is this guy?' I ask. 'I keep hearing his name bandied about.'

'No one really knows, but Hester is obsessed with him,' scoffs Sadie.

I glance at her. Sounds like someone's a bit jealous. What's going on there?

Floss's phone vibrates, and she clicks into the message and squeals loudly.

I flinch, and Damian almost drops his blood bag. 'Ow!' he says, rubbing his left ear. As newbies, our hearing is supersensitive.

'Sorry, babe.'

'Did she get it?' I ask.

'She says, "Ask Damian if hypnosis can help someone get over stage fright."'

Damian grins. 'I think that's a "yes" then.'

Floss's phone rings, and she puts it on speaker. 'Did you get it? Did you get the part?' she asks breathlessly.

There's a pause, and Hester says, 'I just found out ... I got it.'

We all whoop and clap and call out 'Congratulations!'

Hester laughs. 'Thanks, guys. I'm flying back up tonight so we can celebrate. And discuss you-know-what.'

Smiling, I look around, but Sadie has disappeared. Fuck it. She's driving me batty. I can't wait any longer. I need to do this right now. I should've when we first got back, but I chickened out.

I walk into the kitchen to find her boiling the kettle and spooning coffee into a mug. I lean against the door, watching her.

'Is that for me?'

'Hah, yeah. Old habits die hard.'

She takes the kitchen knife and starts to draw it across her wrist.

'Wait,' I say, walking over and staying her hand. I take it

in mine and drop to one knee.

'Sadie Bouffant. I've loved you for forty years.'

She looks at me, expressionless. 'Elliott, don't ...'

'Let me finish. Please,' I beg. 'I've got a small speech that I've prepared.'

Her eyelids flutter, but she nods, and I steel myself. Where was I? Oh yes.

'I've loved you for forty years. To steal Jerry Maguire's line, "You complete me."' I do the hand sign as well since she's made me watch the movie with her at least a hundred times. Sadie's mouth twitches. I stumble on.

'I know it's corny, but it's exactly how I feel. I want to spend eternity with you. Will you do me the very great honour of becoming my wife?'

My voice wobbles, but I manage to get it all out without stammering. Thank God vampires can't cry, or I'd be a blubbering mess right now. With my free hand, I take a black velvet box out of my pocket and present it to her. It contains a Georgian rose-gold engagement ring set with a small emerald.

'I found it in an antique store a few years ago and I've been waiting for the right moment. I know how much you love emeralds ...'

I trail off as Sadie stares first at me, and then at the ring.

She doesn't speak for a long moment, and I realise too late that I shouldn't have done this in the kitchen. It's exactly like Tim's proposal.

She's going to reject me. I've fucked it up!

Then Sadie gives a small smile, which keeps getting bigger until it lights up her beautiful face. She cups my cheeks in her hands and gives me a long, slow kiss.

'Is that a "yes"?' I ask, worried that it's a 'no' and this is her way of letting me down gently.

'Of course it's a "yes",' she says softly. 'I've loved you for decades. Why do you think I kept you as my thrall all these years?'

'Because you needed an on-site snack?'

She laughs and shakes her head as I slide the emerald ring onto her finger. It fits perfectly!

Sadie's eyes turn serious as she inspects her emerald ring from all angles. 'This is truly beautiful, Elliott. I love it, thank you so much. But your timing is atrocious.'

'Oh, why?'

'Because as you said quite recently, "*we have to go to London and stake a vampire.*" And I don't particularly want to get engaged if there's a chance you might not make it back for the wedding.'

'Ah, true.' That's a sobering thought that she thinks I

won't. So much for greater strength in numbers.

Sadie grins. 'I'm joking.'

I drag a hand through my hair. 'That's a fucking relief.'

'Though I do have one condition for marrying you.'

'Which is?'

'That I can walk down the aisle to "Hungry Like the Wolf".'

I rise and sweep her up into my arms with a laugh.

'Sweetheart', I growl, nuzzling her neck and never wanting to let her go, 'you can walk down the aisle to any goddamn Duran Duran song you like!'

Sadie squeals with delight and almost butchers my eardrums, causing the rest of the flat to come rushing into the kitchen.

'What the fuck is going on? We thought you were being drained!' cries Floss.

Sadie laughs. She holds up her left hand and wiggles her fingers. 'Not drained. Engaged! Elliott proposed, and I accepted!'

This elicits more squealing for my ears to contend with from Floss, as well as excited clapping. Damian pumps my hand, wincing as well, but yells 'Congrats, mate!'

I watch as Sadie hugs Floss gleefully and my undead heart brims with joy and love. It's all been worth it for this moment. To see her so happy. She's hidden it well over the years, but now I know the truth: my brave, funny, strong girl may be steel on the outside, but inside, she's soft, gooey marshmallow where I'm concerned.

Harlot, coven protector, mistress, blood bank CEO—Sadie has worn many hats over the centuries, some of which I witnessed firsthand as her thrall—but now I'm thrilled we're moving forward, preparing for our new future as vampire husband and wife. Whatever hardships lie ahead, Sadie and I will face them together.

I'm bitten, completely smitten, and I'm planning on us being together forever. Fingers—and fangs—crossed!

TO BE CONTINUED...

Find out what happens next in Book 3
Biting My Knight – Hester and Will's story and
the Fanged and Flirty finale!

Books by Angela

FANGED AND FLIRTY SERIES

Flossed In Love

Enthralled By You

MISS AUSTEN SERIES

Trusting Miss Austen

Visiting Miss Austen

Amusing Miss Austen

STANDALONES

POX

Brontë Lovers

The Holly Project

You Had Me at Ice Cream

I'll Meet You in Florence

The House of Dating Disasters

My Double Life

Travel & Mayhem

COLLECTIONS

3 Book Rom-Com Collection

Miss Austen Series Box Set

All books available on Amazon and Kindle Unlimited

Acknowledgements

Thank you for reading *Enthralled By You*. I hope you enjoyed it as much as I did writing it! If so, I'd be thrilled if you left a review or star rating on Amazon and/or Goodreads.

I'm so grateful for having a team of people to help me on the publishing journey. Thank you to my beta readers, Jessica Taylor and Chris Lambert, for their insights and encouraging comments. Big thanks also to my diligent copy editor, Peachy Yap, and to My Lan Khuc Valle for her gorgeous cover art!

Check out the *Enthralled By You* Spotify playlist at

➔ angelapearse.pub/book-spotify-playlists

Join my mailing list for new releases,
offers, and bookish news!

➔ angelapearse.pub

About the Author

ANGELA PEARSE writes contemporary, historical, and paranormal romances. Known for her quirky humour, Angela's books are often described as 'page-turners', ranging from light-hearted escapades to darker satire.

A freelance editor with an MA in English, Angela is originally from New Zealand but now calls Edinburgh home, finding endless inspiration in its rich history and atmospheric streets. Visit angelapearse.pub for more information or to join her mailing list.